James Russell Lowell, Mabel Caldwell Willard

James Russell Lowell's Vision of Sir Launfal

James Russell Lowell, Mabel Caldwell Willard

James Russell Lowell's Vision of Sir Launfal

ISBN/EAN: 9783337342463

Printed in Europe, USA, Canada, Australia, Japan

Cover: Foto ©Andreas Hilbeck / pixelio.de

More available books at **www.hansebooks.com**

JAMES RUSSELL LOWELL'S

VISION OF SIR LAUNFAL

AND

OTHER POEMS

EDITED BY

MABEL CALDWELL WILLARD

INSTRUCTOR IN LITERATURE, NEW HAVEN, CONN.

LEACH, SHEWELL, & SANBORN,

BOSTON.   NEW YORK.   CHICAGO.

TYPOGRAPHY BY C. J. PETERS & SON, BOSTON.
PRESSWORK BY BERWICK & SMITH.

PREFACE.

JAMES RUSSELL LOWELL stands among the foremost of American poets: — perhaps the majority of scholars would say, that for range of subject, for power and grace of expression, and for poetic insight and spiritual vision, he stands as the foremost of American poets.

It was, therefore, a wise decision that placed *The Vision of Sir Launfal*, one of the most poetic of Lowell's poems, on the list of requirements in English literature for entrance to our colleges.

It has been the endeavor in this edition to make the Notes and Questions of such a nature as will help the student, — first, to get the truth which the poet would teach; and, second, to see the beauty of the poetic language, music, and figure, and their relation to the thought.

The thanks of the editor are due to Prof. Katharine Lee Bates, of Wellesley College, who has kindly allowed her "Hints on the Handling of a Poem," which forms part of the Introduction to her edition of Coleridge's _Ancient Mariner_, to be reprinted here.

For the use of some of the facts in the Biographical Sketch, acknowledgment is here made to Mr. Francis H. Underwood's _Biographical Sketch of James Russell Lowell._

MABEL CALDWELL WILLARD.

NEW HAVEN, CONN.,
November, 1896.

CONTENTS.

INTRODUCTION.

I. SKETCH OF LOWELL'S LIFE. (1819-1891.)

JAMES RUSSELL LOWELL came from a Massachusetts family descended from Percival Lowell of Bristol, England, who came to New England in 1639, and settled in Newbury.

The family, as far back as can be traced, has been eminent for those characteristics of great intelligence, rare ability, and high moral worth, which distinguish only the truly great.

Lowell's grandfather, John Lowell, drafted the clause in the Constitution of Massachusetts by which slavery was brought to its end in that State.

His father was a clergyman in Boston for over fifty years; his mother, who was Harriet Traill Spence before her marriage, was of Scotch descent, and it was from her that the son inherited his imaginative, poetic nature.

Four children preceded James Russell, who was born on the 22d of February, 1819, at "Elmwood," Cambridge,—where, in the same house, seventy-two years later, he passed on into the higher life.

"Elmwood" is a beautiful, old New England place, with ample grounds studded with large fine elms.

The influence of his environment is most forcibly seen in his writings. His poems are crowded with similes and metaphors taken from Nature, and show him to have been, not

1

merely a close observer of her, but a friend who entered into
warmest sympathy with her every mood.

His father's library contained an excellent collection of
miscellaneous works; and here the boy browsed, and fed, and
cultivated his taste with biographies, travels, and classics from
the English and French. When he was sixteen he entered
Harvard College; but distinguished himself more by his in-
difference to the prescribed studies than by his attainments
in them.

He himself has frankly confessed that he would never have
been allowed to take his degree had it not been that he was
his father's son. It is pleasant to remember, and perhaps
consoling to some youthful minds to think, that in years after
he became a professor in this same University, and received
honorary degrees from the Universities of Oxford and Cambridge, England.

His negligence of the college curriculum. of which he re-
pented in later days, was, however, more than compensated
for, in the way of literary culture, by his great love for reading, and the excellent judgment which he exercised in satisfy-
ing this love.

In 1844 he married Miss Maria White, the influence of
whose pure and beautiful character upon the young man was
most ennobling and permanent. His own innate nobility and
beauty of soul received through her a stimulus and inspiration
which never left him.

At "Elmwood" still hang their portraits, painted by William Page. "She, with refined features, transparent skin,
starry blue eyes, and smooth bands of light brown hair: he.
with serious face and eyes in shadow, with ruddy, wavy. and
glossy auburn hair falling almost to the shoulders, a full,

reddish beard, wearing a coarse-textured brown coat, and a broad linen collar turned carelessly down. There are few modern portraits in which costume counts for so little, and soul for so much."

The social life became to him from this time forth a medium through which his spiritual nature might work for the ennobling of his fellow-beings.

It is interesting to note that it was soon after his marriage that the following poem, *Sir Launfal*, was written. No one can read his poetry without being impressed by his consecration to all that is pure and just and holy. His efforts were always in behalf of freedom, love of man, and love of Christ.

In the *Biglow Papers*, two series, the first published in 1848, and the second during the Civil War, 1861–1866, he enlisted himself in the anti-slavery cause — a cause which in those early days was a most unpopular one, even in the North.

In 1851 and 1852 he spent some time travelling in Europe with his wife, whose health was growing constantly more frail. In 1853 this wife, in whose fellowship there had been such rare inspiration, passed on into the unseen world — and yet we cannot feel that there was any real separation, for to one of his beautiful sonnets we listen with bowed head, hearing words which tell of his heart's history : —

"Love hath so purified my being's core,
  Meseems I scarcely should be startled, even,
  To find, some morn, that thou hadst gone before,
  Since, with thy love, this knowledge too was given,
  Which each calm day doth strengthen more and more,
  That they who love are but one step from Heaven."

In 1855 he succeeded Longfellow as professor of Modern Languages and Literature at Harvard College.

In 1857 he became editor of the *Atlantic Monthly*; this office he filled for about five years, and then, for the next ten years, held a similar position on the *North American Review*. It was in the same year in which he undertook the editorship of the *Atlantic Monthly* that he was married to Miss Frances Dunlap, a woman of prepossessing qualities of mind and person.

He was United States Minister to Spain in 1877, and from 1880 to 1885 United States Minister to England. In his capacity as foreign minister, especially in Great Britain, where he was much longer than in Spain, he held a most enviable place in the esteem and regard of the Queen and her subjects. Here, as everywhere, he was always a most loyal American. His patriotism never allowed him to swerve from his democratic principles, and his loyalty to high ideals kept him singularly free from the slightest subserviency to a desire for fame.

Besides his poems he published at various times essays — *Among my Books*, and *My Study Windows*; and addresses, both literary and political. Lowell's prose is clear, often brilliant, and always delightful.

But it is as a poet pre-eminently that we love and admire him. Perhaps to no other American is the name of poet more truly applicable, although he himself most generously and admiringly shared it with Longfellow, Whittier, Bryant, and Holmes.

His sense of humor is most happy; it was by the use of the humorous element, rather than the serious, that he did his most effective work for the anti-slavery cause.

He had a love for Nature, both intense and deep; as with Wordsworth, she was to him a living, breathing soul. His

own words express this attitude towards her more perfectly
than can any one else : —

> "An' th' airth don't git put out with me
> *That love her's though she was a woman.*"

But although a poet of Nature, he is still more the poet of
Man; the weak and the oppressed found in him a courageous
and impassioned spokesman; he feared no censure nor scorn
that his allegiance to the slave might bring him; he longed
only to break his chains, and to help bring the happy day
when each man should look upon his neighbor, whether of
high or low degree, as his brother.

He is even more deeply the poet of Love. His poems which
have love for their theme are less numerous than the others,
but they are quite as profound, and reach even more nearly
to the core of the man's heart. It was through this love,
which so influenced and held his life, that he became the
champion of the weak and downtrodden.

> "That love for one, from which there doth not spring
> Wide love for all, is but a worthless thing.
> Not in another world, as poets prate,
> Dwell we apart above the tide of things,
> High floating o'er earth's clouds on faery wings;
> But our pure love doth ever elevate
> Into a holy bond of brotherhood
> All earthly things, making them pure and good."

And it was through this sweet human love that there entered into his life the consecration to the Love which is the
source of all happiness and noble living. In his poem entitled
The Search, he has expressed it thus : —

"So from my feet the dust
    Of the proud World I shook;
Then came dear Love and shared with me his crust,
    And half my sorrow's burden took.
    After the World's soft bed,
    Its rich and dainty fare,
Like down seemed Love's coarse pillow to my head,
    His cheap food seemed as manna rare;
Fresh-trodden prints of bare and bleeding feet,
    Turned to the heedless city whence I came,
Hard by I saw, and springs of worship sweet
    Gushed from my cleft heart smitten by the same;
Love looked me in the face and spake no words,
But straight I knew those footprints were the Lord's.

    "I followed where they led,
    And in a hovel rude,
With naught to fence the weather from his head,
The King I sought for meekly stood;
    A naked, hungry child
    Clung round his gracious knee,
And a poor hunted slave looked up and smiled
    To bless the smile that set him free;
New miracles I saw his presence do, —
    No more I knew the hovel bare and poor,
The gathered chips into a woodpile grew,
    The broken morsel swelled to goodly store;
I knelt and wept: my Christ no more I seek,
His throne is with the outcast and the weak."

All of his poems are fraught with this deeply religious element. The spiritual life was the only *real* life to him : —

    "O Power, more near my life than life itself."

There was in it no moroseness or narrowness; it was as
broad and deep and joyous as the sunshine; it was as clear

and happy as the song of birds; and it was surer than his
very life — nay, it was his very life.

> "O Power, more near my life than life itself
> (Or what seems life to us in sense immured),
> Even as the roots, shut in the darksome earth,
> Share in the tree-top's joyance, and conceive
> Of sunshine and wide air and wingèd things
> By sympathy of nature, so do I
> Have evidence of Thee so far above,
> Yet in and of me! Rather Thou the root
> Invisibly sustaining, hid in light,
> Not darkness, or in darkness made by us.
> If sometimes I must hear good men debate
> Of other witness of Thyself than Thou,
> As if there needed any help of ours
> To nurse Thy flickering life, that else must cease,
> Blown out, as 'twere a candle, by men's breath,
> My soul shall not be taken in their snare,
> To change her inward surety for their doubt
> Muffled from sight in formal robes of proof:
> While she can only feel herself through Thee,
> I fear not Thy withdrawal; more I fear,
> Seeing, to know Thee not, hoodwinked with dreams
> Of signs and wonders, while, unnoticed, Thou,
> Walking Thy garden still, commun'st with men,
> Missed in the commonplace of miracle."

II. LOWELL'S LITERARY STYLE.

If faultless verse were the one requisite of poetry, then we
should not be able to give to Lowell, one of our sweetest and
truest melodists, the name of poet. But if, as Stopford Brooke
says, "poetry is an art, and the artist in poetry is the one who
writes for pure pleasure and for nothing else the thing he
writes, and who desires to give to others the same fine pleas-

ure by his poems which he had in writing them,"—and since
highest pleasure can come only through true, and noble, and
joyous life,—then Lowell, whose poems are full of inspiration
to such life, must take the highest rank among our home poets
—must take, at times, rank with the best poets of the English
language.

Stopford Brooke goes on, however, to say that the thing
the poet "most cares about is that the form in which he puts
his thoughts or feelings may be perfectly fitting to the subject,
and as beautiful as possible." Here Lowell finds his limita-
tions; here he falls short of always ranking among the best
poets. Either he does not care sufficiently that his "form"
"may be as beautiful as possible," or he is unable to clothe
his thought in its most beautiful garb. But considering the
beauty of his thought, and at times the beauty of his form,
he is always a poet,—sometimes a poet of highest rank.

Although occasionally we can trace a happy similarity between his style and that of some other writer, yet he is never
a copyist, only an appreciative admirer of the poet in ques-
tion; his style is always his own.

Sometimes it is stately and dignified, but oftener quick and
joyous in movement, as though brain and heart were so full
of thoughts, and beautiful imagery for them, that the hand
could not be timed in expressing them. He is always simple
and earnest; seldom is the impression made of studied effect,
either in grace or dignity. And the style is the exponent of
the man; the simple, eager, childlike of heart, but noble and
gracious man, is as much revealed to us through his mode
of expression, as by the thoughts themselves. And in his
simplicity and naturalness lies one of the chief charms of
his style. It is only in rare and unfortunate instances that

we detect an effort after the elaborate; as a rule no word is added which might have been left out, no thought introduced which wearies by reiteration. This earnestness of style is made emphatic by a clear and vigorous mode of expression.

His figures, drawn largely from nature, have the tone and color of life, and are always in harmony with the thought.

There is no one, perhaps, who has more deliciously blended wit and humor than Lowell; his humor is as sweet as Chaucer's, but more rollicking; his wit as keen and pointed as the sharpest arrow-tip, but never moistened with the smallest drop of poison. Underneath the wit and humor one feels the kindly heart which has reverence for every human soul, although exposing so ruthlessly the follies and weaknesses which too often hinder and warp those souls.

Although not a dramatist, yet he has held the mirror up to the face of man so steadily, that we see reflected the features of many faces in outlines clear and distinct.

III. LITERARY ESTIMATES OF LOWELL.

" With such a genius for comedy, — greater, I believe, than any English poet ever had, — with such wit, drollery, Yankee sense and spirit, I wonder he does not see his ·best hold,' and stick to it."   THACKERAY.

" If we look at certain grave, sweet pages of Thackeray, Newman, Martineau, Matthew Arnold, and the Ruskin of thirty·years ago, we feel that we have in them specimens of ideal English. Something of the calm dignity, the seemingly artless perfection, and the limpid movement, characteristic of those writers, may sometimes be seen in passages of Lowell;

but his felicity in figures, and the irrepressible rush of his double stream of thought, often lead him into a style of writing that is both poetry and prose, and is not purely either. . . .

"If the soul of poetry is energy, its garment beauty, its effect emotion; if, according to Landor, 'philosophy should run through poetry as veins do through the body'; if that is a poem which is inspired with original thought, graced by unborrowed pictures and figures, and which suggests continually more than meets the eye, — then it will be impossible to deny Lowell a high rank among poets. . . .

"Poems with such a range, such vivid conceptions, such high purpose, such keen insight, such tender sympathy, and such flashing lights of imagery, have never been very common."

FRANCIS H. UNDERWOOD, LL.D.

"There is no historic circle of wits and scholars, not that of Beaumont and Ben Jonson where, haply, Shakespeare sat, nor Pope's, nor Dryden's, nor Addison's, nor Dr. Johnson's Club, nor that of Edinburgh; nor any Parisian *salon* or German study, to which Lowell's abundance would not have contributed a golden drop, and his glancing wit a glittering repartee." [On his prose.] "Racy and rich, and often of the most sonorous or delicate cadence, it is still the prose of a poet and a master of the differences of form. His prose indeed is often profoundly poetic — that is, quick with imagination, but always in the form of prose, not of poetry. It is so finely compact of illustration, of thought and learning, of wit and fancy and permeating humor, that his prose page sparkles and sways like a phosphorescent sea."

GEORGE WILLIAM CURTIS.

"The style of Mr. Lowell is emphatically his own, and yet no man reports so habitually — half sympathetically, half whimsically — the ring of other writers. Homer Wilbur is especially redolent or resonant of the old Elizabethan masters.

"We hear the grave Verulam Lord Bacon, or the judicious Hooker. . . . Sometimes we get an odd flavor of Swift, bright humor being substituted for malignant satire; at others, the flowing and tender style of Jeremy Taylor comes back to us as we read. . . .

"Yet is he as voluminous and many-sided in poetry as in prose; 'he sings to one clear harp in divers tones.'"

H. R. HAWEIS.

"As often as the first eight lines of this poem [*The Vision of Sir Launfal*] come to mind, I feel a poetic breath not borne to me again from our home hills and fields, and rarely wafted from the old lands beyond the sea; and passing on to the thirty-third line beginning,

'And what is so rare as a day in June?'

I say each time, 'Here and in certain passages of the later odes are the purest, the sweetest, and at the same time the freshest strains from any singer of our soil.'"

JOHN VANCE CHENEY.

IV. HINTS ON THE HANDLING OF A POEM.

(From PROF. KATHARINE LEE BATES'S edition of COLERIDGE'S *Ancient Mariner.*)

"POETRY," says Coleridge, "is the blossom and the fragrance of all human knowledge, human thoughts, human passions, emotions, language."

Essentially a poem cannot be taught. The student learns his deepest lesson from the poet and from no other. A teacher does well to be on his guard, lest he obtrude his own personality between the two. It is the poet himself, who, arresting the attention by song, holding it by vision after vision, can best impart to the young intellect the truth he has to tell, can alone inspire in the young heart a sympathetic passion for that truth. The function of the teacher, in dealing with any particular poem, is, first and foremost, to help the student fix his attention upon it. This can usually be done by questioning, better than in any other way. A running fire of questions, searching, varied, stimulates the mental activity, pricks into life the sluggish perceptions, gives form and color to those poem-pictures which are often so dimly and vaguely reproduced by the untutored imagination; and thus securing the vivid presentment of the scene, the clear comprehension of the thought, does away with the intellectual barrier, and brings the heart of the student into free contact with the glowing heart of the poet. Since definite knowledge is a requisite basis for true sympathy, such questions would relate in part to the meaning of terms and phrases employed; and rigid must be the will of that teacher who is not sometimes tempted aside from his main object by the "fossil poetry" of individual words, and led to inquire into the secrets of their origin and growth; yet the study of literature is more than philology. Such questions might relate, in part, to the structure of sentences; the significance of allusions, geographical, historical, mythological; the value of an illustration; the force of an argument; the development of a thought; — all this to insure a firm intellectual grasp of the subject-matter. Yet this done, the half has not been done. To understand the poet's message is one thing; to feel it, know it, and reach out beyond it toward the purer message he suggests, but has not words to utter, is another. Indeed, care should constantly be taken that these more superficial questions be kept in the background and not suffered to distract the student's mind from the poetic essence. For the study of literature must not be mistaken for the study of syntax, geography, history, mythology, or logic. All questions that awaken the imagination and enable it to glorify the printed words into such clear-colored visions as dazzled the " mind's eye " of the poet while he wrote are of peculiar value. Questions that quicken the ear to the music of the poet's verse, and all other questions that render the student aware of poetic artifice, responsive to poetic effects, indirectly serve to deepen the central impression of the poem ; since these very melodies and rhetorical devices are not idle ornament, but the studied emphasis of the poet's word. Questions that lead the student to recognize and define in himself the emotions aroused by one passage or another in the poem, questions that call forth an attempt to supply missing links in the chain of events, questions that carry the reason and imagination forward on the lines suggested by the poet, all tend to mould the student's mood into sympathy with that higher mood, sensitive, eager, impassioned, in which the singer first conceived his song.

The question-method may be well supplemented by topical recitation, class discussion, citation of parallel passages, comparison with kindred poems and, under due precautions, the reading of criticisms. The committing a poem to memory, that its virtue may gradually distil into the mind and become a force in the unconscious life, is most desirable wherever it is possible to train the student to learn poetry by heart and not by rote. The slavish and mechanical engrossing of words, lines, and stanzas upon some blank tablet of the brain, is of questionable benefit; but where the student is able to learn the poem as a *poem*, not as a column of verses, — to possess himself, by the powers of attention and analysis, of the sequence of events and grouping of images, remembering these in the poet's own language, because on trial he finds that language the most natural and best; this surpasses for poetic education every exercise that the ingenuity of teacher can devise.

At all events, leave the student alone with the poet at the first and at the last. Let him have his earliest reading of the poem with fresh, unprejudiced mind, and when teacher, classroom, and critics have done their best and their worst with him, return him to the poet again. If possible, let a little time intervene, and then let the poem be read aloud before the class; or, better still, recited by some one who has entered deeply into its spirit, and whose voice is musical and expressive. So will the first impression be intensified, and the seed-sowing of analysis and criticism be harvested in a richer renewal of poetic sympathy. For poetry is not knowledge to be apprehended; it is passion to be felt. — passion for the truth revealed in beauty, and for the hinted truth too beautiful to be revealed."

THE VISION OF SIR LAUNFAL.

PRELUDE TO PART FIRST.

I.

OVER his keys the musing organist,
　Beginning doubtfully and far away,
First lets his fingers wander as they list,
　And builds a bridge from Dreamland for his lay:
Then, as the touch of his loved instrument
　Gives hope and fervor, nearer draws his theme,
First guessed by faint auroral flushes sent
　Along the wavering vista of his dream.

II.

　Not only around our infancy
　Doth heaven with all its splendors lie;　　　**10**
　Daily, with souls that cringe and plot,
　We Sinais climb and know it not.

III

Over our manhood bend the skies;
　Against our fallen and traitor lives

15

The great winds utter prophecies;
　　With our faint hearts the mountain **strives**;
Its arms outstretched, the druid wood
　　Waits with its benedicite;
And to our age's drowsy blood
　　Still shouts the inspiring sea.   **20**

IV.

Earth gets its price for what Earth gives us;
　　The beggar is taxed for a corner to die in,
The priest hath his fee who comes and shrives us,
　　We bargain for the graves we lie in;
At the devil's booth are all things sold,
Each ounce of dross costs its ounce of gold;
　　For a cap and bells our lives we pay,
Bubbles we buy with a whole soul's tasking:
　　'Tis heaven alone that is given away,
'Tis only God may be had for the asking;   **30**
No price is set on the lavish summer;
June may be had by the poorest comer.

V.

And what is so rare as a day in June?
　　Then, if ever, come perfect days;
Then Heaven tries earth if it be in tune,
　　And over it softly her warm ear lays:
Whether we look, or whether we listen,
We hear life murmur, or see it glisten;
Every clod feels a stir of might,

An instinct within it that reaches and towers,　　40
And, groping blindly above it for light,
　　Climbs to a soul in grass and flowers;
The flush of life may well be seen
　　Thrilling back over hills and valleys;
The cowslip startles in meadows green,
　　The buttercup catches the sun in its chalice,
And there's never a leaf nor a blade too mean
　　To be some happy creature's palace;
The little bird sits at his door in the sun,
　　Atilt like a blossom among the leaves,　　50
And lets his illumined being o'errun
　　With the deluge of summer it receives;
His mate feels the eggs beneath her wings,
And the heart in her dumb breast flutters and sings;
He sings to the wide world, and she to her nest, —
In the nice ear of Nature which song is the best?

VI.

Now is the high-tide of the year,
　　And whatever of life hath ebbed away
Comes flooding back with a ripply cheer
　　Into every bare inlet and creek and bay;　　60
Now the heart is so full that a drop overfills it,
We are happy now because God wills it;
No matter how barren the past may have been,
'Tis enough for us now that the leaves are green;
We sit in the warm shade and feel right well
How the sap creeps up and the blossoms swell;

We may shut our eyes, but we cannot help knowing
That skies are clear and grass is growing;
The breeze comes whispering in our ear
That dandelions are blossoming near,   70
    That maize has sprouted, that streams are flowing, ,
That the river is bluer than the sky,
That the robin is plastering his house hard by;
And if the breeze kept the good news back,
For other couriers we should not lack;
    We could guess it all by yon heifer's lowing, —
And hark! how clear bold chanticleer,
Warmed with the new wine of the year,
    Tells all in his lusty crowing!

                    VII.

Joy comes, grief goes, we know not how;   80
Everything is happy now,
    Everything is upward striving;
'Tis as easy now for the heart to be true
As for grass to be green or skies to be blue, —
    'Tis the natural way of living:
Who knows whither the clouds have fled?
    In the unscarred heaven they leave no wake;
And the eyes forget the tears they have shed,
    The heart forgets its sorrow and ache;
The soul partakes the season's youth,   90
    And the sulphurous rifts of passion and woe
Lie deep 'neath a silence pure and smooth,
    Like burnt-out craters healed with snow.

What wonder if Sir Launfal now
Remembered the keeping of his vow ?

PART FIRST.

I.

" My golden spurs now bring to me,
    And bring to me my richest mail,
For to-morrow I go over land and sea
    In search of the Holy Grail ;
Shall never a bed for me be spread,   100
Nor shall a pillow be under my head,
Till I begin my vow to keep ;
Here on the rushes will I sleep,
And perchance there may come a vision true
Ere day create the world anew."
    Slowly Sir Launfal's eyes grew dim,
    Slumber fell like a cloud on him,
And into his soul the vision flew.

II.

The crows flapped over by twos and threes,
In the pool drowsed the cattle up to their knees,   110
    The little birds sang as if it were
    The one day of summer in all the year,
And the very leaves seemed to sing on the trees :
The castle alone in the landscape lay
Like an outpost of winter, dull and gray ;
'Twas the proudest hall in the North Countree,

And never its gates might opened be,
Save to lord or lady of high degree;
Summer besieged it on every side,
But the churlish stone her assaults defied;   120
She could not scale the chilly wall,
Though around it for leagues her pavilions tall
Stretched left and right.
Over the hills and out of sight;
    Green and broad was every tent,
    And out of each a murmur went
Till the breeze fell off at night.

III.

The drawbridge dropped with a surly clang,
And through the dark arch a charger sprang,
Bearing Sir Launfal, the maiden knight,   130
In his gilded mail, that flamed so bright
It seemed the dark castle had gathered all
Those shafts the fierce sun had shot over its wall
    In his siege of three hundred summers long,
And, binding them all in one blazing sheaf,
    Had cast them forth: so, young and strong,
And lightsome as a locust-leaf,
Sir Launfal flashed forth in his maiden mail,
To seek in all climes for the Holy Grail.

IV.

It was morning on hill and stream and tree,   140
    And morning in the young knight's heart;

Only the castle moodily
Rebuffed the gifts of the sunshine free,
And gloomed by itself apart;
The season brimmed all other things up
Full as the rain fills the pitcher-plant's cup.

V.

As Sir Launfal made morn through the darksome gate,
He was 'ware of a leper, crouched by the same,
Who begged with his hand and moaned as he sate;
And a loathing over Sir Launfal came;   150
The sunshine went out of his soul with a thrill,
The flesh 'neath his armor 'gan shrink and crawl,
And midway its leap his heart stood still
Like a frozen waterfall;
For this man, so foul and bent of stature,
Rasped harshly against his dainty nature,
And seemed the one blot on the summer morn, —
So he tossed him a piece of gold in scorn.

VI.

The leper raised not the gold from the dust:
" Better to me the poor man's crust,   160
Better the blessing of the poor,
Though I turn me empty from his door;
That is no true alms which the hand can hold;
He gives only the worthless gold
Who gives from a sense of duty:
But he who gives but a slender mite,

And gives to that which is out of sight,
  That thread of the all-sustaining Beauty
Which runs through all and doth all unite, —
The hand cannot clasp the whole of his alms.   170
The heart outstretches its eager palms,
For a god goes with it and makes it store
To the soul that was starving in darkness before."

PRELUDE TO PART SECOND.

1.

Down swept the chill wind from the mountain peak,
  From the snow five thousand summers old ;
On open wold and hill-top bleak
  It had gathered all the cold,
And whirled it like sleet on the wanderer's cheek ;
It carried a shiver everywhere
From the unleafed boughs and pastures bare ;   180
The little brook heard it and built a roof
'Neath which he could house him, winter-proof ;
All night by the white stars' frosty gleams
He groined his arches and matched his beams ;
Slender and clear were his crystal spars
As the lashes of light that trim the stars :
He sculptured every summer delight
In his halls and chambers out of sight ;
Sometimes his tinkling waters slipt
Down through a frost-leaved forest-crypt,   190
Long, sparkling aisles of steel-stemmed trees

Bending to counterfeit a breeze;
Sometimes the roof no fretwork knew
But silvery mosses that downward grew;
Sometimes it was carved in sharp relief
With quaint arabesques of ice-fern leaf;
Sometimes it was simply smooth and clear
For the gladness of heaven to shine through, and here
He had caught the nodding bulrush-tops
And hung them thickly with diamond drops,   200
That crystalled the beams of moon and sun,
And made a star of every one:
No mortal builder's most rare device
Could match this winter-palace of ice;
'Twas as if every image that mirrowed lay
In his depths serene through the summer day,
Each fleeting shadow of earth and sky,
    Lest the happy model should be lost,
Had been mimicked in fairy masonry
    By the elfin builders of the frost.   210

II.

Within the hall are song and laughter,
    The cheeks of Christmas glow red and jolly,
And sprouting is every corbel and rafter
    With lightsome green of ivy and holly;
Through the deep gulf of the chimney wide
Wallows the Yule-log's roaring tide;
The broad flame-pennons droop and flap
    And belly and tug as a flag in the wind;

Liks a locust shrills the imprisoned sap,
  Hunted to death in its galleries blind;   220
And swift little troops of silent sparks,
  Now pausing. now scattering away as in fear,
Go threading the soot-forest's tangled darks
  Like herds of startled deer.

III.

But the wind without was eager and sharp,
Of Sir Launfal's gray hair it makes a harp,
    And rattles and wrings
    The icy strings.
  Singing, in dreary monotone,
  A Christmas carol of its own,   230
  Whose burden still, as he might guess,
  Was — " Shelterless, shelterless, shelterless!"
The voice of the seneschal flared like a torch
As he shouted the wanderer away from the porch,
And he sat in the gateway and saw all night
  The great hall-fire, so cheery and bold,
  Through the window-slits of the castle old,
Build out its piers of ruddy light
Against the drift of the cold.

PART SECOND.

I.

There was never a leaf on bush or tree,   240
The bare boughs rattled shudderingly;

The river was dumb and could not speak,
  For the weaver Winter its shroud had spun;
A single crow on the tree-top bleak
  From his shining feathers shed off the cold sun;
Again it was morning, but shrunk and cold,
As if her veins were sapless and old,
And she rose up decrepitly
For a last dim look at earth and sea.

II.

Sir Launfal turned from his own hard gate,   250
For another heir in his earldom sate;
An old, bent man, worn out and frail,
He came back from seeking the Holy Grail;
Little he recked of his earldom's loss,
No more on his surcoat was blazoned the cross
But deep in his soul the sign he wore,
The badge of the suffering and the poor.

III.

Sir Launfal's raiment thin and spare
Was idle mail 'gainst the barbed air.
For it was just at the Christmas time;   260
So he mused, as he sat, of a sunnier clime,
And sought for a shelter from cold and snow
In the light and warmth of long-ago;
He sees the snake-like caravan crawl
O'er the edge of the desert, black and small,
Then nearer and nearer, till, one by one,

He can count the camels in the sun,
As over the red-hot sands they pass
To where, in its slender necklace of grass,
The little spring laughed and leapt in the shade,   270
And with its own self like an infant played,
And waved its signal of palms.

IV.

" For Christ's sweet sake, I beg an alms ; " —
The happy camels may reach the spring,
But Sir Launfal sees only the grewsome thing,
The leper, lank as the rain-blanched bone,
That cowers beside him, a thing as lone
And white as the ice-isles of Northern seas,
In the desolate horror of his disease.

V

And Sir Launfal said, — " I behold in thee   280
An image of Him who died on the tree;
Thou also hast had thy crown of thorns, —   .
Thou also hast had the world's buffets and scorns, —
And to thy life were not denied
The wounds in the hands and feet and side :
Mild Mary's Son, acknowledge me ;
Behold, through him, I give to thee ! "

VI.

Then the soul of the leper stood up in his eyes
    And looked at Sir Launfal, and straightway he

Remembered in what a haughtier guise   290
    He had flung an alms to leprosie,
When he girt his young life up in gilded mail
And set forth in search of the Holy Grail.
The heart within him was ashes and dust;
He parted in twain his single crust,
He broke the ice on the streamlet's brink,
And gave the leper to eat and drink,
'Twas a mouldy crust of coarse brown bread,
    'Twas water out of a wooden bowl, —
Yet with fine wheaten bread was the leper fed,   300
    And 'twas red wine he drank with his thirsty soul

VII.

As Sir Launfal mused with a downcast face,
A light shone round about the place;
The leper no longer crouched at his side,
But stood before him glorified,
Shining and tall and fair and straight
As the pillar that stood by the Beautiful Gate, —
Himself the Gate whereby men can
Enter the temple of God in Man.

VIII.

His words were shed softer than leaves from the pine,
And they fell on Sir Launfal as snows on the brine,   311
That mingle their softness and quiet in one
With the shaggy unrest they float down upon;
And the voice that was softer than silence said,

"Lo it is I, be not afraid !
In many climes, without avail,
Thou hast spent thy life for the Holy Grail ;
Behold, it is here, — this cup which thou
Didst fill at the streamlet for me but now ;
This crust is my body broken for thee,   320
This water his blood that died on the tree ;
The Holy Supper is kept, indeed,
In whatso we share with another's need ;
Not what we give, but what we share,
For the gift without the giver is bare ;
Who gives himself with his alms feeds three,
Himself, his hungering neighbor, and me."

IX.

Sir Launfal awoke as from a swound :
"The Grail in my castle here is found
Hang my idle armor up on the wall,   330
Let it be the spider's banquet-hall ;
He must be fenced with stronger mail
Who would seek and find the Holy Grail."

X.

The castle gate stands open now,
   And the wanderer is welcome to the hall
As the hangbird is to the elm-tree bough ;
   No longer scowl the turrets tall,
The Summer's long siege at last is o'er ;
When the first poor outcast went in at the door,

She entered with him in disguise,   340
And mastered the fortress by surprise;
There is no spot she loves so well on ground,
She lingers and smiles there the whole year round;
The meanest serf on Sir Launfal's land
Has hall and bower at his command;
And there's no poor man in the North Countree
But is lord of the earldom as much as he.

NOTE. — According to the mythology of the Romancers, the San
Greal, or Holy Grail, was the cup out of which Jesus partook of the
Last Supper with his disciples. It was brought into England by
Joseph of Arimathea, and remained there, an object of pilgrimage
and adoration, for many years in the keeping of his lineal descen-
dants. It was incumbent upon those who had charge of it to be
chaste in thought, word, and deed; but one of the keepers having
broken this condition, the Holy Grail disappeared. From that time
it was a favorite enterprise of the knights of Arthur's court to go in
search of it. Sir Galahad was at last successful in finding it, as may
be read in the seventeenth book of the *Romance of King Arthur*.
Tennyson has made Sir Galahad the subject of one of the most ex-
quisite of his poems.

The plot (if I may give that name to anything so slight) of the
foregoing poem is my own, and, to serve its purposes, I have en-
larged the circle of competition in search of the miraculous cup in
such a manner as to include, not only other persons than the heroes
of the Round Table, but also a period of time subsequent to the sup-
posed date of King Arthur's reign.

PROMETHEUS.

One after one the stars have risen and set,
Sparkling upon the hoarfrost on my chain :
The Bear, that prowled all night about the fold
Of the North-star, hath shrunk into his den,
Scared by the blithesome footsteps of the Dawn,
Whose blushing smile floods all the Orient;
And now bright Lucifer grows less and less,
Into the heaven's blue quiet deep-withdrawn.
Sunless and starless all, the desert sky
Arches above me, empty as this heart   10
For ages hath been empty of all joy,
Except to brood upon its silent hope,
As o'er its hope of day the sky doth now.
All night have I heard voices : deeper yet
The deep low breathing of the silence grew,
While all about, muffled in awe, there stood
Shadows, or forms, or both, clear-felt at heart,
But, when I turned to front them, far along
Only a shudder through the midnight ran,
And the dense stillness walled me closer round.   20
But still I heard them wander up and down
That solitude, and flappings of dusk wings
Did mingle with them, whether of those hags
Let slip upon me once from Hades deep,
Or of yet direr torments, if such be,
I could but guess ; and then toward me came

A shape as of a woman: very pale
It was, and calm; its cold eyes did not move,
And mine moved not, but only stared on them.
Their fixèd awe went through my brain like ice; 30
A skeleton hand seemed clutching at my heart,
And a sharp chill, as if a dank night fog
Suddenly closed me in, was all I felt:
And then, methought, I heard a freezing sigh,
A long, deep, shivering sigh, as from blue lips
Stiffening in death, close to mine ear. I thought
Some doom was close upon me, and I looked
And saw the red moon through the heavy mist,
Just setting, and it seemed as it were falling,
Or reeling to its fall, so dim and dead 40
And palsy-struck it looked. Then all sounds merged
Into the rising surges of the pines,
Which, leagues below me, clothing the gaunt loins
Of ancient Caucasus with hairy strength,
Sent up a murmur in the morning wind,
Sad as the wail that from the populous earth
All day and night to high Olympus soars,
Fit incense to thy wicked throne, O Jove!

Thy hated name is tossed once more in scorn
From off my lips, for I will tell thy doom. 50
And are these tears? Nay, do not triumph, Jove!
They are wrung from me but by the agonies
Of prophecy, like those sparse drops which fall
From clouds in travail of the lightning, when

The great wave of the storm high-curled and black
Rolls steadily onward to its thunderous break.
Why art thou made a god of, thou poor type
Of anger, and revenge, and cunning force ?
True Power was never born of brutish Strength,
Nor sweet Truth suckled at the shaggy dugs   60
Of that old she-wolf. Are thy thunderbolts,
That quell the darkness for a space. so strong
As the prevailing patience of meek Light,
Who, with the invincible tenderness of peace,
Wins it to be a portion of herself ?
Why art thou made a god of, thou, who hast
The never-sleeping terror at thy heart,
That birthright of all tyrants, worse to bear
Than this thy ravening bird on which I smile ?
Thou swear'st to free me if I will unfold   70
What kind of doom it is whose omen flits
Across thy heart, as o'er a troop of doves
The fearful shadow of the kite. What need
To know that truth whose knowledge cannot save ?
Evil its errand hath, as well as Good ;
When thine is finished, thou art known no more :
There is a higher purity than thou,
And higher purity is greater strength ,
Thy nature is thy doom, at which thy heart
Trembles behind the thick wall of thy might.   80
Let man but hope, and thou art straightway chilled
With thought of that drear silence and deep night
Which, like a dream. shall swallow thee and thine :

Let man but will, and thou art god no more,
More capable of ruin than the gold
And ivory that image thee on earth.
He who hurled down the monstrous Titan-brood
Blinded with lightnings, with rough thunders stunned,
Is weaker than a simple human thought.   .
My slender voice can shake thee, as the breeze,   90
That seems but apt to stir a maiden's hair,
Sways huge Oceanus from pole to pole;
For I am still Prometheus, and foreknow
In my wise heart the end and doom of all.

Yes, I am still Prometheus, wiser grown
By years of solitude, — that holds apart
The past and future, giving the soul room
To search into itself, — and long commune
With this eternal silence; — more a god,
In my long-suffering and strength to meet   100
With equal front the direst shafts of fate,
Than thou in thy faint-hearted despotism,
Girt with thy baby-toys of force and wrath.
Yes, I am that Prometheus who brought down
The light to man, which thou, in selfish fear,
Hadst to thyself usurped, — his by sole right,
For Man hath right to all save Tyranny, —
And which shall free him yet from thy frail throne.
Tyrants are but the spawn of Ignorance,
Begotten by the slaves they trample on,   110
Who, could they win a glimmer of the light,

And see that Tyranny is always weakness,
Or Fear with its own bosom ill at ease,
Would laugh away in scorn the sand-wove chain
Which their own blindness feigned for adamant.
Wrong ever builds on quicksands, but the Right
To the firm centre lays its moveless base.
The tyrant trembles, if the air but stir
The innocent ringlets of a child's free hair,
And crouches, when the thought of some great spirit, 120
With world-wide murmur, like a rising gale,
Over men's hearts, as over standing corn,
Rushes, and bends them to its own strong will.
So shall some thought of mine yet circle earth,
And puff away thy crumbling altars, Jove !

And, wouldst thou know of my supreme revenge,
Poor tyrant, even now dethroned in heart,
Realmless in soul, as tyrants ever are,
Listen ! and tell me if this bitter peak,
This never-glutted vulture, and these chains   130
Shrink not before it ; for it shall befit
A sorrow-taught, unconquered Titan-heart.
Men, when their death is on them, seem to stand
On a precipitous crag that overhangs
The abyss of doom, and in that depth to see,
As in a glass, the features dim and vast
Of things to come, the shadows, as it seems,
Of what have been.   Death ever fronts the wise;
Not fearfully, but with clear promises

Of larger life, on whose broad vans upborne,   140
Their outlook widens, and they see beyond
The horizon of the Present and the Past,
Even to the very source and end of things.
Such am I now : immortal woe hath made
My heart a seer, and my soul a judge
Between the substance and the shadow of Truth.
The sure supremeness of the Beautiful,
By all the martyrdoms made doubly sure
Of such as I am, this is my revenge,
Which of my wrongs builds a triumphal arch.   150
Through which I see a sceptre and a throne,
The pipings of glad shepherds on the hills,
Tending the flocks no more to bleed for thee, —
The songs of maidens pressing with white feet
The vintage on thine altars poured no more, —
The murmurous bliss of lovers, underneath
Dim grapevine bowers, whose rosy bunches press
Not half so closely their warm cheeks, unpaled
By thoughts of thy brute lust, — the hive-like hum
Of peaceful commonwealths, where sunburnt Toil   160
Reaps for itself the rich earth made its own
By its own labor, lightened with glad hymns
To an omnipotence which thy mad bolts
Would cope with as a spark with the vast sea, —
Even the spirit of free love and peace,
Duty's sure recompense through life and death, —
These are such harvests as all master-spirits
Reap, haply not on earth, but reap no less

Because the sheaves are bound by hands not **theirs** ;
These are the bloodless daggers wherewithal   170
They stab fallen tyrants, this their high revenge :
For their best part of life on earth is when,
Long after death, prisoned and pent no more,
Their thoughts, their wild dreams even, have become
Part of the necessary air men breathe :
When, like the moon, herself behind a cloud,
They shed down light before us on life's sea,
That cheers us to steer onward still in hope.
Earth with her twining memories ivies o'er
Their holy sepulchres ; the chainless sea,   180
In tempest or wide calm, repeats their thoughts ;
The lightning and the thunder, all free things,
Have legends of them for the ears of men.
All other glories are as falling stars,
But universal Nature watches theirs :
Such strength is won by love of human kind.

Not that I feel that hunger after fame,
Which souls of a half-greatness are beset with ;
But that the memory of noble deeds
Cries shame upon the idle and the vile,   190
And keeps the heart of Man forever up
To the heroic level of old time.
To be forgot at first is little pain
To a heart conscious of such high intent
As must be deathless on the lips of men ;
But, having been a name, to sink and be

A something which the world can do without,
Which, having been or not, would never change
The lightest pulse of fate, — this is indeed
A cup of bitterness the worst to taste,   200
And this thy heart shall empty to the dregs.
Endless despair shall be thy Caucasus,
And memory thy vulture ; thou wilt find
Oblivion far lonelier than this peak.
Behold thy destiny !   Thou think'st it much
That I should brave thee, miserable god !
But I have braved a mighter than thou,
Even the tempting of this soaring heart,
Which might have made me, scarcely less than thou,
A god among my brethren weak and blind,   210
Scarce less than thou, a pitiable thing
To be down-trodden into darkness soon.
But now I am above thee, for thou art
The bungling workmanship of fear, the block
The awes the swart Barbarian ; but I
Am what myself have made, — a nature wise
With finding in itself the types of all,
With watching from the dim verge of the time
What things to be are visible in the gleams
Thrown forward on them from the luminous past,   220
Wise with the history of its own frail heart,
With reverence and with sorrow, and with love,
Broad as the world, for freedom and for man.

Thou and all strength shall crumble, except Love,

By whom, and for whose glory, ye shall cease:
And, when thou'rt but a weary moaning heard
From out the pitiless gloom of Chaos, I
Shall be a power and a memory,
A name to fright all tyrants with, a light
Unsetting as the pole-star, a great voice   230
Heard in the breathless pauses of the fight
By truth and freedom ever waged with wrong,
Clear as a silver trumpet, to awake
Far echoes that from age to age live on
In kindred spirits, giving them a sense
Of boundless power from boundless suffering wrung:
And many a glazing eye shall smile to see
The memory of my triumph (for to meet
Wrong with endurance, and to overcome
The present with a heart that looks beyond,   240
Are triumph), like a prophet eagle, perch
Upon the sacred banner of the Right.
Evil springs up, and flowers, and bears no seed,
And feeds the green earth with its swift decay,
Leaving it richer for the growth of truth ;
But Good, once put in action or in thought,
Like a strong oak, doth from its boughs shed down
The ripe germs of a forest.   Thou, weak god,
Shalt fade and be forgotten ! but this soul,
Fresh-living still in the serene abyss,   250
In every heaving shall partake, that grows
From heart to heart among the sons of men, —
As the ominous hum before the earthquake runs

Far through the Ægean from roused isle to isle, —
Foreboding wreck to palaces and shrines,
And mighty rents in many a cavernous error
That darkens the free light to man : — This heart,
Unscarred by thy grim vulture, as the truth
Grows but more lovely 'neath the beaks and claws
Of Harpies blind that fain would soil it, shall   260
In all the throbbing exultations share
That wait on freedom's triumphs, and in all
The glorious agonies of martyr-spirits,
Sharp lightning-throes to split the jagged clouds
That veil the future, showing them the end,
Pain's thorny crown for constancy and truth,
Girding the temples like a wreath of stars.
This is a thought, that, like the fabled laurel,
Makes my faith thunder-proof ; and thy dread bolts
Fall on me like the silent flakes of snow   270
On the hoar brows of aged Caucasus :
But, oh thought far more blissful, they can rend
This cloud of flesh, and make my soul a star !

  Unleash thy crouching thunders now, O Jove !
Free this high heart, which, a poor captive long,
Doth knock to be let forth, this heart which still,
In its invincible manhood, overtops
Thy puny godship, as this mountain doth
The pines that moss its roots.   O, even now,
While from my peak of suffering I look down,   280
Beholding with a far-spread gush of hope

The sunrise of that Beauty, in whose face,
Shone all around with love, no man shall look
But straightway like a god he be uplift
Unto the throne long empty for his sake,
And clearly oft foreshadowed in brave dreams
By his free inward nature, which nor thou,
Nor any anarch after thee, can bind
From working its great doom, — now, now set free
This essence, not to die, but to become   290
Part of that awful Presence which doth haunt
The palaces of tyrants, to scare off,
With its grim eyes and fearful whisperings
And hideous sense of utter loneliness,
All hope of safety, all desire of peace,
All but the loathed forefeeling of blank death, —
Part of that spirit which doth ever brood
In patient calm on the unpilfered nest
Of man's deep heart, till mighty thoughts grow fledged
To sail with darkening shadow o'er the world,   300
Filling with dread such souls as dare not trust
In the unfailing energy of Good,
Until they swoop, and their pale quarry make
Of some o'erbloated wrong, — that spirit which
Scatters great hopes in the seed-field of man,
Like acorns among grain, to grow and be
A roof for freedom in all coming time!

But no, this cannot be ; for ages yet,
In solitude unbroken, shall I hear

The angry Caspian to the Euxine shout,   310
And Euxine answer with a muffled roar,
On either side storming the giant walls
Of Caucasus with leagues of climbing foam
(Less, from my height, than flakes of downy snow),
That draw back baffled but to hurl again,
Snatched up in wrath and horrible turmoil,
Mountain on mountain, as the Titans erst,
My brethren, scaling the high seat of Jove,
Heaved Pelion upon Ossa's shoulders broad
In vain emprise. The moon will come and go   320
With her monotonous vicissitude;
Once beautiful, when I was free to walk
Among my fellows, and to interchange
The influence benign of loving eyes,
But now by aged use grown wearisome; —
False thought! most false! for how could I endure
These crawling centuries of lonely woe
Unshamed by weak complaining, but for thee,
Loneliest, save me, of all created things,
Mild-eyed Astarte, my best comforter,   330
With thy pale smile of sad benignity?

    Year after year will pass away and seem
To me, in mine eternal agony,
But as the shadows of dumb summer clouds,
Which I have watched so often darkening o'er
The vast Sarmatian plain, league-wide at first,
But, with still swiftness, lessening on and on

Till cloud and shadow meet and mingle where
The gray horizon fades into the sky,
Far, far to northward. Yes, for ages yet   340
Must I lie here upon my altar huge,
A sacrifice for man. Sorrow will be,
As it hath been, his portion; endless doom,
While the immortal with the mortal linked
Dreams of its wings and pines for what it dreams,
With upward yearn unceasing. Better so:
For wisdom is stern sorrow's patient child,
And empire over self, and all the deep
Strong charities that make men seem like gods;
And love, that makes them be gods, from her breasts   350
Sucks in the milk that makes mankind one blood.
Good never comes unmixed, or so it seems,
Having two faces, as some images
Are carved, of foolish gods; one face is ill;
But one heart lies beneath, and that is good,
As are all hearts, when we explore their depths.
Therefore, great heart, bear up! thou art but type
Of what all lofty spirits endure, that fain
Would win men back to strength and peace through love:
Each hath his lonely peak, and on each heart   360
Envy, or scorn, or hatred, tears lifelong
With vulture beak; yet the high soul is left;
And faith, which is but hope grown wise, and love
And patience which at last shall overcome.

1843.

THE PRESENT CRISIS.

I.

WHEN a deed is done for Freedom, through the broad
earth's aching breast
Runs a thrill of joy prophetic, trembling on from east to
west,
And the slave, where'er he cowers, feels the soul within
him climb
To the awful verge of manhood, as the energy sublime
Of a century bursts full-blossomed on the thorny stem of
Time.

II.

Through the walls of hut and palace shoots the instan-
taneous throe,
When the travail of the Ages wrings earth's systems to
and fro ;
At the birth of each new Era, with a recognizing start,
Nation wildly looks at nation, standing with mute lips
apart,
And glad Truth's yet mightier man-child leaps beneath
the Future's heart.   10

III.

So the Evil's triumph sendeth, with a terror and a
chill,
Under continent to continent, the sense of coming ill,

And the slave, where'er he cowers, feels his sympathies
    with God
In hot tear-drops ebbing earthward, to be drunk up by
    the sod,
Till a corpse crawls round unburied, delving in the
    nobler clod.

IV.

For mankind are one in spirit, and an instinct bears
    along,
Round the earth's electric circle, the swift flash of right
    or wrong;
Whether conscious or unconscious, yet Humanity's vast
    frame
Through its ocean-sundered fibres feels the gush of joy
    or shame; —
In the gain or loss of one race all the rest have equal
    claim.   20

V.

Once to every man and nation comes the moment to
    decide,
In the strife of Truth with Falsehood, for the good or
    evil side;
Some great cause, God's new Messiah, offering each the
    bloom or blight,
Parts the goats upon the left hand, and the sheep upon
    the right,
And the choice goes by forever 'twixt that darkness and
    .that light.

VI.

Hast thou chosen, O my people, on whose party thou
shalt stand,
Ere the Doom from its worn sandals shakes the dust
against our land ?
Though the cause of Evil prosper, yet 'tis Truth alone
is strong,
And, albeit she wander outcast now, I see around her
throng
Troops of beautiful, tall angels, to enshield her from all
wrong.   30

VII.

Backward look across the ages and the beacon-moments
see,
That, like peaks of some sunk continent, jut through
Oblivion's sea ;
Not an ear in court or market for the low foreboding
cry
Of those Crises, God's stern winnowers, from whose feet
earth's chaff must fly ;
Never shows the choice momentous till the judgment
hath passed by.

VIII.

Careless seems the great Avenger ; history's pages but
record
One death-grapple in the darkness 'twixt old systems
and the Word ;

Truth forever on the scaffold, Wrong forever on the
    throne, —
Yet that scaffold sways the future, and, behind the dim
    unknown,
Standeth God within the shadow, keeping watch above
    his own.   40

IX.

We see dimly in the Present what is small and what is
    great.
Slow of faith, how weak an arm may turn the iron helm
    of fate,
But the soul is still oracular; amid the market's din,
List the ominous stern whisper from the Delphic cave
    within, —
" They enslave their children's children who make com-
    promise with sin."

X.

Slavery, the earth-born Cyclops, fellest of the giant
    brood,
Sons of brutish Force and Darkness. who have drenched
    the earth with blood.
Famished in his self-made desert, blinded by our purer
    day,
Gropes in yet unblasted regions for his miserable
    prey ; —
Shall we guide his gory fingers where our helpless chil-
    dren play ?   50

XI.

Then to side with Truth is noble when we share her
    wretched crust,
Ere her cause bring fame and profit, and 'tis prosperous
    to be just;
Then it is the brave man chooses, while the coward
    stands aside,
Doubting in his abject spirit, till his Lord is cruci-
    fied,
And the multitude make virtue of the faith they had
    denied.

XII.

Count me o'er earth's chosen heroes, — they were souls
    that stood alone,
While the men they agonized for hurled the contume-
    lious stone,
Stood serene, and down the future saw the golden beam
    incline
To the side of perfect justice, mastered by their faith
    divine,
By one man's plain truth to manhood and to God's
    supreme design.   60

XIII.

By the light of burning heretics Christ's bleeding feet I
    track,
Toiling up new Calvaries ever with the cross that turns
    not back,

And these mounts of anguish number how each genera-
  tion learned
One new word of that grand *Credo* which in prophet-
  hearts hath burned
Since the first man stood God-conquered with his face
  to heaven upturned.

XIV.

For Humanity sweeps onward : where to-day the martyr
  stands,
On the morrow crouches Judas with the silver in his
  hands ;
Far in front the cross stands ready and the crackling
  fagots burn,
While the hooting mob of yesterday in silent awe return
To glean up the scattered ashes into History's golden
  urn.   70

XV.

'Tis as easy to be heroes as to sit the idle slaves
Of a legendary virtue carved upon our fathers' graves,
Worshippers of light ancestral make the present light a
  crime ; —
Was the Mayflower launched by cowards, steered by
  men behind their time ?
Turn those tracks toward Past or Future, that make
  Plymouth Rock sublime ?

XVI.

They were men of present valor, stalwart old icono-
 clasts,
Unconvinced by axe or gibbet that all virtue was the
 Past's;
But we make their truth our falsehood, thinking that
 hath made us free,
Hoarding it in mouldy parchments, while our tender
 spirits flee
The rude grasp of that great Impulse which drove them
 across the sea.   80

XVII.

They have rights who dare maintain them; we are
 traitors to our sires,
Smothering in their holy ashes Freedom's new-lit altar
 fires;
Shall we make their creed our jailer? Shall we, in our
 haste to slay,
From the tombs of the old prophets steal the funeral
 lamps away
To light up the martyr-fagots round the prophets of
 to-day?

XVIII.

New occasions teach new duties; Time makes ancient
 good uncouth;
They must upward still, and onward, who would keep
 abreast of Truth;

Lo, before us gleam her camp-fires! we ourselves must
    Pilgrims be,
Launch our Mayflower, and steer boldly through the
    desperate winter sea,
Nor attempt the Future's portal with the Past's blood-
    rusted key.   90

December, 1844.   ————

THE FATHERLAND.

I.

Where is the true man's fatherland?
   Is it where he by chance is born?
   Doth not the yearning spirit scorn
In such scant borders to be spanned?
O yes! his fatherland must be
As the blue heaven wide and free!

II.

Is it alone where freedom is,
   Where God is God and man is man?
   Doth he not claim a broader span
For the soul's love of home than this?   10
O yes! his fatherland must be
As the blue heaven wide and free!

III.

Where'er a human heart doth wear
   Joy's myrtle-wreath or sorrow's gyves,

Where'er a human spirit strives
After a life more true and fair,
There is the true man's birthplace grand,
His is a world-wide fatherland!

IV.

Where'er a single slave doth pine,
   Where'er one man may help another, —   20
   Thank God for such a birthright, brother, —
That spot of earth is thine and mine!
There is the true man's birthplace grand,
His is a world-wide fatherland

AN INDIAN-SUMMER REVERIE.

I.

WHAT visionary tints the year puts on,
When falling leaves falter through motionless air
   Or numbly cling and shiver to be gone!
How shimmer the low flats and pastures bare,
   As with her nectar Hebe Autumn fills
   The bowl between me and those distant hills,
And smiles and shakes abroad her misty, tremulous hair!

II.

No more the landscape holds its wealth apart,
Making me poorer in my poverty,
   But mingles with my senses and my heart;   10

My own projected spirit seems to me
  In her own reverie the world to steep;
  'Tis she that waves to sympathetic sleep,
Moving, as she is moved, each field and hill and tree.

III.

How fuse and mix, with what unfelt degrees,
  Clasped by the faint horizon's languid arms,
  Each into each, the hazy distances!
The softened season all the landscape charms;
  Those hills, my native village that embay,
  In waves of dreamier purple roll away,   20
And floating in mirage seem all the glimmering farms.

IV.

Far distant sounds the hidden chickadee
Close at my side; far distant sound the leaves;
  The fields seem fields of dream, where Memory
Wanders like gleaning Ruth; and as the sheaves
  Of wheat and barley wavered in the eye
  Of Boaz as the maiden's glow went by,
So tremble and seem remote all things the sense receives.

V.

The cock's shrill trump that tells of scattered corn,
Passed breezily on by all his flapping mates,   30
  Faint and more faint, from barn to barn is borne,
Southward, perhaps to far Magellan's Straits;

Dimly I catch the throb of distant flails;
Silently overhead the hen-hawk sails,
With watchful, measuring eye, and for his quarry waits.

VI.

The sobered robin, hunger-silent now,
Seeks cedar-berries blue, his autumn cheer;
    The chipmunk, on the shingly shagbark's bough,
Now saws, now lists with downward eye and ear,
    Then drops his nut, and, cheeping, with a bound   40
    Whisks to his winding fastness underground;
The clouds like swans drift down the streaming atmos-
        phere.

VII.

O'er you bare knoll the pointed cedar shadows
Drowse on the crisp, gray moss; the ploughman's call
    Creeps faint as smoke from black, fresh-furrowed
        meadows;
The single crow a single caw lets fall;
    And all around me every bush and tree
    Says Autumn's here, and Winter soon will be,
Who snows his soft, white sleep and silence over all.

VIII.

The birch, most shy and ladylike of trees,   50
Her poverty, as best she may, retrieves,
    And hints at her foregone gentilities

With some saved relics of her wealth of leaves;
  The swamp-oak, with his royal purple on,
  Glares red as blood across the sinking sun,
As one who proudlier to a falling fortune cleaves.

IX.

He looks a sachem, in red blanket wrapt,
  Who, mid some council of the sad-garbed whites,
  Erect and stern, in his own memories lapt,
  With distant eye broods over other sights,   60
    Sees the hushed wood the city's flare replace,
    The wounded turf heal o'er the railway's trace,
And roams the savage Past of his undwindled rights.

X.

The red-oak, softer-grained, yields all for lost,
  And, with his crumpled foliage stiff and dry,
  After the first betrayal of the frost,
  Rebuffs the kiss of the relenting sky;
    The chestnuts, lavish of their long-hid gold,
    To the faint Summer, beggared now and old,
Pour back the sunshine hoarded 'neath her favoring
    eye.   70

XI.

The ash her purple drops forgivingly
  And sadly, breaking not the general hush;
  The maple-swamps glow like a sunset sea,

Each leaf a ripple with its separate flush;
    All round the wood's edge creeps the skirting blaze
    Of bushes low, as when, on cloudy days,
Ere the rain fall, the cautious farmer burns his brush.

XII.

    O'er you low wall, which guards one unkempt zone,
Where vines and weeds and scrub-oaks intertwine
    Safe from the plough, whose rough, discordant
        stone   80
Is massed to one soft gray by lichens fine,
    The tangled blackberry, crossed and recrossed,
        weaves
    A prickly network of ensanguined leaves;
Hard by, with coral beads, the prim black-alders shine.

XIII.

    Pillaring with flame this crumbling boundary,
Whose loose blocks topple 'neath the ploughboy's foot,
    Who, with each sense shut fast except the eye,
Creeps close and scares the jay he hoped to shoot,
    The woodbine up the elm's straight stem aspires.
    Coiling it, harmless, with autumnal fires;   90
In the ivy's paler blaze the martyr oak stands mute.

XIV.

    Below, the Charles — a stripe of nether sky,
Now hid by rounded apple-trees between,

Whose gaps the misplaced sail sweeps bellying by,
Now flickering golden through a woodland screen,
  Then spreading out, at his next turn beyond,
  A silver circle like an inland pond —
Slips seaward silently through marshes purple and
    green.

XV.

Dear marshes! vain to him the gift of sight
Who cannot in their various incomes share,   100
  From every season drawn, of shade and light,
  Who sees in them but levels brown and bare;
  Each change of storm or sunshine scatters free
  On them its largess of variety,
For Nature with cheap means still works her wonders
    rare.

XVI.

In Spring they lie one broad expanse of green,
O'er which the light winds run with glimmering feet:
  Here, yellower stripes track out the creek unseen,
  There, darker growths o'er hidden ditches meet;
  And purpler stains show where the blossoms crowd,
  As if the silent shadow of a cloud   111
Hung there becalmed, with the next breath to fleet.

XVII.

All round, upon the river's slippery edge,
Witching to deeper calm the drowsy tide,

Whispers and leans the breeze-entangling sedge;
Through emerald glooms the lingering waters slide,
Or, sometimes wavering, throw back the sun,
And the stiff banks in eddies melt and run
Of dimpling light, and with the current seem to glide.

XVIII.

In Summer 'tis a blithesome sight to see,   120
As, step by step, with measured swing, they pass,
The wide-ranked mowers wading to the knee,
Their sharp scythes panting through the wiry grass;
Then, stretched beneath a rick's shade in a ring,
Their nooning take, while one begins to sing
A stave that droops and dies 'neath the close sky of
brass.

XIX.

Meanwhile that devil-may-care, the bobolink,
Remembering duty, in mid-quaver stops
Just ere he sweeps o'er rapture's tremulous brink,
And 'twixt the winrows most demurely drops,   130
A decorous bird of business, who provides
For his brown mate and fledglings six besides,
And looks from right to left, a farmer mid his crops.

XX.

Another change subdues them in the Fall,
But saddens not; they still show merrier tints,

Though sober russet seems to cover all;
When the first sunshine through their dew-drops
glints,
Look how the yellow clearness, streamed across,
Redeems with rarer hues the season's loss,
As Dawn's feet there had touched and left their rosy
prints.   140

XXI.

Or come when sunset gives its freshened zest,
Lean o'er the bridge and let the ruddy thrill,
While the shorn sun swells down the hazy west,
Glow opposite; — the marshes drink their fill
And swoon with purple veins, then slowly fade
Through pink to brown, as eastward moves the
shade,
Lengthening with stealthy creep, of Simond's darken-
ing hill.

XXII.

Later, and yet ere Winter wholly shuts,
Ere through the first dry snow the runner grates,
And the loath cart-wheel screams in slippery
ruts,   150
While firmer ice the eager boy awaits,
Trying each buckle and strap beside the fire,
And until bedtime plays with his desire,
Twenty times putting on and off his new-bought
skates; —

XXIII.

Then, every morn, the river's banks shine bright
With smooth plate-armor, treacherous and frail,
 By the frost's clinking hammers forged at night,
'Gainst which the lances of the sun prevail,
 Giving a pretty emblem of the day
 When guiltier arms in light shall melt away, 160
And states shall move free-limbed, loosed from war's
   cramping mail.

XXIV.

And now those waterfalls the ebbing river
Twice every day creates on either side
 Tinkle, as through their fresh-sparred grots they
   shiver
In grass-arched channels to the sun denied;
 High flaps in sparkling blue the far-heard crow,
 The silvered flats gleam frostily below,
Suddenly drops the gull and breaks the glassy tide.

XXV.

But crowned in turn by vying seasons three,
Their winter halo hath a fuller ring; 170
 This glory seems to rest immovably, —
The others were too fleet and vanishing;
 When the hid tide is at its highest flow,
 O'er marsh and stream one breathless trance of
   snow
With brooding fulness awes and hushes everything.

XXVI.

The sunshine seems blown off by the bleak wind,
As pale as formal candles lit by day ;
　　Gropes to the sea the river dumb and blind;
The brown ricks, snow-thatched by the storm in play,
　　Show pearly breakers combing o'er their lee,　　180
　　White crests as of some just enchanted sea,
Checked in their maddest leap and hanging poised midway.

XXVII.

But when the eastern blow, with rain aslant,
From mid-sea's prairies green and rolling plains
　　Drives in his wallowing herds of billows gaunt,
And the roused Charles remembers in his veins
　　Old Ocean's blood and snaps his gyves of frost,
　　That tyrannous silence on the shores is tost
In dreary wreck, and crumbling desolation reigns.

XXVIII.

Edgewise or flat, in Druid-like device,　　190
With leaden pools between or gullies bare,
　　The blocks lie strewn, a bleak Stonehenge of ice;
No life, no sound, to break the grim despair,
　　Save sullen plunge, as through the sedges stiff
　　Down crackles riverward some thaw-sapped cliff,
Or when the close-wedged fields of ice crunch here and there.

XXIX.

But let me turn from fancy-pictured scenes
To that whose pastoral calm before me lies:
  Here nothing harsh or rugged intervenes;
The early evening with her misty dyes   200
  Smooths off the ravelled edges of the nigh,
  Relieves the distant with her cooler sky,
And tones the landscape down, and soothes the wearied
    eyes.

XXX.

There gleams my native village, dear to me,
Though higher change's waves each day are seen,
  Whelming fields famed in boyhood's history,
Sanding with houses the diminished green;
  There, in red brick, which softening time defies,
  Stand square and stiff the Muses' factories; —
How with my life knit up is every well-known scene!   210

XXXI.

Flow on, dear river! not alone you flow
To outward sight, and through your marshes wind;
  Fed from the mystic springs of long-ago,
Your twin flows silent through my world of mind:
  Grow dim, dear marshes, in the evening's gray!
  Before my inner sight ye stretch away,
And will forever, though these fleshly eyes grow blind.

XXXII.

Beyond the hillock's house-bespotted swell,
Where Gothic chapels house the horse and chaise,
Where quiet cits in Grecian temples dwell,   220
Where Coptic tombs resound with prayer and praise,
Where dust and mud the equal year divide,
There gentle Allston lived, and wrought, and died,
Transfiguring street and shop with his illumined gaze.

XXXIII.

Virgilium vidi tantum, — I have seen
But as a boy, who looks alike on all,
That misty hair, that fine Undine-like mien,
Tremulous as down to feeling's faintest call ; —
Ah, dear old homestead ! count it to thy fame   ·
That thither many times the Painter came ; —   230
One elm yet bears his name, a feathery tree and tall.

XXXIV.

Swiftly the present fades in memory's glow, —
Our only sure possession is the past ;
The village blacksmith died a month ago,
And dim to me the forge's roaring blast ;
Soon fire-new mediævals we shall see
Oust the black smithy from its chestnut-tree,
And that hewn down, perhaps, the bee-hive green and
vast.

XXXV.

How many times, prouder than king on throne,
Loosed from the village school-dame's A's and B's, 240
Panting have I the creaky bellows blown,
And watched the pent volcano's red increase,
  Then paused to see the ponderous sledge, brought
    down
  By that hard arm voluminous and brown,
From the white iron swarm its golden vanishing bees.

XXXVI.

Dear native town! whose choking elms each year
With eddying dust before their time turn gray,
  Pining for rain, — to me thy dust is dear;
It glorifies the eve of summer day,
  And when the westering sun half sunken burns, 250
  The mote-thick air to deepest orange turns,
The westward horseman rides through clouds of gold
    away,

XXXVII.

So palpable, I've seen those unshorn few,
The six old willows at the causey's end
  (Such trees Paul Potter never dreamed nor drew),
Through this dry mist their checkering shadows send,
  Striped, here and there, with many a long-drawn
    thread,
  Where streamed through leafy chinks the trembling
    red,

Past which, in one bright trail, the hangbird's flashes
    blend.

XXXVIII.

Yes, dearer far thy dust than all that e'er,   260
  Beneath the awarded crown of victory,
    Gilded the blown Olympic charioteer;
  Though lightly prized the ribboned parchments three,
    Yet *collegisse juvat*, I am glad
    That here what colleging was mine I had, —
It linked another tie, dear native town, with thee!

XXXIX.

Nearer art thou than simply native earth,
  My dust with thine concedes a deeper tie;
    A closer claim thy soil may well put forth,
  Something of kindred more than sympathy;   270
    For in thy bounds I reverently laid away
    That blinding anguish of forsaken clay,
That title I seemed to have in earth and sea and sky,

XL.

That portion of my life more choice to me
  (Though brief, yet in itself so round and whole)
    Than all the imperfect residue can be; —
  The Artist saw his statue of the soul
    Was perfect; so, with one regretful stroke,
    The earthen model into fragments broke,
And without her the impoverished seasons roll.   280

SONG.

I.

VIOLET ! sweet violet !
Thine eyes are full of tears ;
    Are they wet
    Even yet
With the thought of other years ?
Or with gladness are they full,
For the night so beautiful,
And longing for those far-off spheres ?

II.

Loved one of my youth thou wast,
Of my merry youth,
    And I see,
    Tearfully,
All the fair and sunny past,
All its openness and truth,
Ever fresh and green in thee
As the moss is in the sea.

III.

Thy little heart, that hath with love
Grown colored like the sky above,
On which thou lookest ever, —

Can it know
All the woe
Of hope for what returneth never,
All the sorrow and the longing
To these hearts of ours belonging?

IV.

Out on it! no foolish pining
For the sky
Dims thine eye,
Or for the stars so calmly shining;
Like thee let this soul of mine
Take hue from that wherefor I long,   30
Self-stayed and high, serene and strong,
Not satisfied with hoping — but divine.

V.

Violet! dear violet!
Thy blue eyes are only wet
With joy and love of Him who sent thee,
And for the fulfilling sense
Of that glad obedience
Which made thee all that Nature meant thee!

1841.

TO THE DANDELION.

I.

DEAR common flower, that grow'st beside the way,
Fringing the dusty road with harmless gold,
    First pledge of blithesome May,
Which children pluck, and, full of pride uphold,
  High-hearted buccaneers, o'erjoyed that they
An Eldorado in the grass have found,
    Which not the rich earth's ample round
May match in wealth, thou art more dear to me
Than all the prouder summer-blooms may be.

II.

Gold such as thine ne'er drew the Spanish prow   10
Through the primeval hush of Indian seas,
    Nor wrinkled the lean brow
Of age, to rob the lover's heart of ease;
  'Tis the Spring's largess, which she scatters now
To rich and poor alike, with lavish hand,
    Though most hearts never understand
  To take it at God's value, but pass by
The offered wealth with unrewarded eye.

III.

Thou art my tropics and mine Italy;
To look at thee unlocks a warmer clime;   20
    The eyes thou givest me.

Are in the heart, and heed not space or time:
  Not in mid June the golden-cuirassed bee
Feels a more summer-like warm ravishment
    In the white lily's breezy tent,
  His fragrant Sybaris, than I. when first
  From the dark green thy yellow circles burst.

IV.

Then think I of deep shadows on the grass,
Of meadows where in sun the cattle graze,
    Where, as the breezes pass.   30
The gleaming rushes lean a thousand ways,
  Of leaves that slumber in a cloudy mass,
Or whiten in the wind, of waters blue
    That from the distance sparkle through
  Some woodland gap, and of a sky above,
Where one white cloud like a stray lamb doth move.

V.

My childhood's earliest thoughts are linked with thee;
The sight of thee calls back the robin's song.
    Who, from the dark old tree
Beside the door, sang clearly all day long,   40
  And I, secure in childish piety,
Listened as if I heard an angel sing
    With news from heaven, which he could bring
  Fresh every day to my untainted ears
When birds and flowers and I were happy peers.

VI.

How like a prodigal doth nature seem,
When thou, for all thy gold, so common art!
    Thou teachest me to deem
More sacredly of every human heart,
    Since each reflects in joy its scanty gleam   50
Of heaven; and could some wondrous secret sho
    Did we but pay the love we owe,
And with a child's undoubting wisdom look
On all these living pages of God's book.

A CHIPPEWA LEGEND.[1]

ἀλγεινὰ μέν μοι καὶ λεγειν ἐστιν ταδε
ἄλγος δὲ σιγᾷν.
        ÆSCHYLUS, *Prom. Vinct.* 197, 198.

I.

The old Chief, feeling now wellnigh his end,
Called his two eldest children to his side,
And gave them, in few words, his parting charge!
"My son and daughter, me ye see no more;
The happy hunting-grounds await me, green
With change of spring and summer through the year:
But, for remembrance, after I am gone,
Be kind to little Sheemah for my sake:
Weakling he is and young, and knows not yet

1 For the leading incidents in this tale, I am indebted to the very valuable *Algic Researches* of Henry R. Schoolcraft, Esq.

To set the trap, or draw the seasoned bow;　　　　10
Therefore of both your loves he hath more need,
And he, who needeth love, to love hath right;
It is not like our furs and stores of corn,
Whereto we claim sole title by our toil,
But the Great Spirit plants it in our hearts,
And waters it, and gives it sun, to be
The common stock and heritage of all:
Therefore be kind to Sheemah, that yourselves
May not be left deserted in your need."

11.

Alone, beside a lake, their wigwam stood,　　　　20
Far from the other dwellings of their tribe
And, after many moons, the loneliness
Wearied the elder brother, and he said,
" Why should I dwell here far from men, shut out
From the free, natural joys that fit my age?
Lo, I am tall and strong, well skilled to hunt,
Patient of toil and hunger, and not yet
Have seen the danger which I dared not look
Full in the face; what hinders me to be
A mighty Brave and Chief among my kin?"　　　　30
So, taking up his arrows and his bow,
As if to hunt, he journeyed swiftly on,
Until he gained the wigwams of his tribe,
Where, choosing out a bride, he soon forgot,
In all the fret and bustle of new life,
The little Sheemah and his father's charge.

III.

Now when the sister found her brother gone,
And that, for many days, he came not back,
She wept for Sheemah more than for herself;
For Love bides longest in a woman's heart,   40
And flutters many times before he flies,
And then doth perch so nearly, that a word
May lure him back to his accustomed nest;
And Duty lingers even when Love is gone,
Oft looking out in hope of his return;
And, after Duty hath been driven forth,
Then Selfishness creeps in the last of all,
Warming her lean hands at the lonely hearth,
And crouching o'er the embers, to shut out
Whatever paltry warmth and light are left,   50
With avaricious greed, from all beside.
So, for long months, the sister hunted wide,
And cared for little Sheemah tenderly;
But, daily more and more, the loneliness
Grew wearisome, and to herself she sighed,
" Am I not fair? at least the glassy pool,
That hath no cause to flatter, tells me so;
But, O, how flat and meaningless the tale,
Unless it tremble on a lover's tongue!
Beauty hath no true glass, except it be   60
In the sweet privacy of loving eyes."
Thus deemed she idly, and forgot the lore
Which she had learned of nature and the woods,
That beauty's chief reward is to itself,

And that Love's mirror holds no image long
Save of the inward fairness, blurred and lost
Unless kept clear and white by Duty's care.
So she went forth and sought the haunts of men,
And, being wedded, in her household cares,
Soon, like the elder brother, quite forgot   70
The little Sheemah and her father's charge.

VI.

But Sheemah, left alone within the lodge,
Waited and waited, with a shrinking heart,
Thinking each rustle was his sister's step,
Till hope grew less and less, and then went out,
And every sound was changed from hope to fear.
Few sounds there were: — the dropping of a nut,
The squirrel's chirrup, and the jay's harsh scream,
Autumn's sad remnants of blithe Summer's cheer,
Heard at long intervals, seemed but to make   80
The dreadful void of silence silenter.
Soon what small store his sister left was gone,
And, through the Autumn, he made shift to live
On roots and berries, gathered in much fear
Of wolves, whose ghastly howl he heard ofttimes,
Hollow and hungry, at the dead of night.
But Winter came at last, and, when the snow,
Thick-heaped for gleaming leagues o'er hill and plain,
Spread its unbroken silence over all,
Made bold by hunger, he was fain to glean   90
(More sick at heart than Ruth, and all alone)

After the harvest of the merciless wolf,
Grim Boaz, who, sharp-ribbed and gaunt, yet feared
A thing more wild and starving than himself;
Till, by degrees, the wolf and he grew friends,
And shared together all the winter through.

V.

 Late in the Spring, when all the ice was gone,
The elder brother, fishing in the lake,
Upon whose edge his father's wigwam stood,
Heard a low moaning noise upon the shore: 100
Half like a child it seemed, half like a wolf,
And straightway there was something in his heart
That said, "It is thy brother Sheemah's voice."
So, paddling swiftly to the bank, he saw,
Within a little thicket close at hand,
A child that seemed fast changing to a wolf,
From the neck downward, gray with shaggy hair,
That still crept on and upward as he looked.
The face was turned away, but well he knew
That it was Sheemah's, even his brother's face.   110
Then with his trembling hands he hid his eyes,
And bowed his head, so that he might not see
The first look of his brother's eyes, and cried,
" O Sheemah! O my brother, speak to me !
Dost thou not know me, that I am thy brother?
Come to me, little Sheemah, thou shalt dwell
With me henceforth, and know no care or want ! "
Sheemah was silent for a space, as if

'Twere hard to summon up a human voice,
And, when he spake, the voice was as a wolf's: 120
" I know thee not, nor art thou what thou say'st;
I have none other brethren than the wolves,
And, till thy heart be changed from what it is,
Thou art not worthy to be called their kin."
Then groaned the other, with a choking tongue,
" Alas! my heart is changed right bitterly;
'Tis shrunk and parched within me even now!"
And, looking upward fearfully, he saw
Only a wolf that shrank away and ran,
Ugly and fierce, to hide among the woods. 130

AMBROSE.

I.

NEVER, surely, was holier man
Than Ambrose, since the world began;
With diet spare and raiment thin
He shielded himself from the father of sin;
With bed of iron and scourgings oft,
His heart to God's hand as wax made soft.

II.

Through earnest prayer and watchings long
He sought to know 'tween right and wrong,

Much wrestling with the blessed Word
To make it yield the sense of the Lord, 10
That he might build a storm-proof creed
To fold the flock in at their need.

III.

At last he builded a perfect faith,
Fenced round about with *The Lord thus saith;*
To himself he fitted the doorway's size,
Meted the light to the need of his eyes,
And knew, by a sure and inward sign,
That the work of his fingers was divine.

IV.

Then Ambrose said, " All those shall die
The eternal death who believe not as I," 20
And some were boiled, some burned in fire,
Some sawn in twain, that his heart's desire,
For the good of men's souls, might be satisfied
By the drawing of all to the righteous side.

V.

One day, as Ambrose was seeking the truth
In his lonely walk, he saw a youth
Resting himself in the shade of a tree;
It had never been granted him to see
So shining a face, and the good man thought
'Twere pity he should not believe as he ought. 30

VI.

So he set himself by the young man's side,
And the state of his soul with questions tried;
But the heart of the stranger was hardened indeed,
Nor received the stamp of the one true creed;
And the spirit of Ambrose waxed sore to find
Such features the porch of so narrow a mind.

VII.

" As each beholds in cloud and fire
The shape that answers his own desire,
So each," said the youth, " in the Law shall find
The figure and fashion of his mind;   40
And to each in his mercy hath God allowed
His several pillar of fire and cloud."

VIII.

The soul of Ambrose burned with zeal
And holy wrath for the young man's weal:
" Believest thou then, most wretched youth,"
Cried he, " a dividual essence in Truth?
I fear me thy heart is too cramped with sin
To take the Lord in his glory in."

IX.

Now there bubbled beside them where they stood
A fountain of waters sweet and good;   50
The youth to the streamlet's brink drew near
Saying, " Ambrose, thou maker of creeds, look here!"

Six vases of crystal then he took,
And set them along the edge of the brook.

X.

" As into these vessels the water I pour,
There shall one hold less, another more,
And the water unchanged, in every case,
Shall put on the figure of the vase ;
O thou, who wouldst unity make through strife,
Canst thou fit this sign to the Water of Life ? "   60

XI.

When Ambrose looked up, he stood alone,
The youth and the stream and the vases were gone ;
But he knew, by a sense of humbled grace,
He had talked with an angel face to face,
And felt his heart change inwardly,
As he fell on his knees beneath the tree.

EXTREME UNCTION.

I.

Go ! leave me, Priest ; my soul would be
    Alone with the consoler, Death ;
Far sadder eyes than thine will see
    This crumbling clay yield up its breath ;

These shrivelled hands have deeper stains
  Than holy oil can cleanse away,
Hands that have plucked the world's coarse gains
  As erst they plucked the flowers of May.

II.

Call, if thou canst, to these gray eyes
  Some faith from youth's traditions wrung;   10
This fruitless husk which dustward dries
  Hath been a heart once, hath been young;
On this bowed head the awful Past
  Once laid its consecrating hands;
The Future in its purpose vast
  Paused, waiting my supreme commands.

III.

But look! whose shadows block the door?
  Who are those two that stand aloof?
See! on my hands this freshening gore
  Writes o'er again its crimson proof!   20
My looked-for death-bed guests are met;
  There my dead Youth doth wring its hands,
And there, with eyes that goad me yet,
  The ghost of my Ideal stands!

IV.

God bends from out the deep and says,
  " I gave thee the great gift of life;
Wast thou not called in many ways?
  Are not my earth and heaven at strife?

I gave thee of my seed to sow,
  Bringest thou me my hundred-fold ? "   30
Can I look up with face aglow,
  And answer, " Father, here is gold " ?

v.

I have been innocent ; God knows
  When first this wasted life began,
Not grape with grape more kindly grows,
  Than I with every brother-man :
Now here I gasp ; what lose my kind,
  When this fast ebbing breath shall part ?
What bands of love and service bind
  This being to a brother heart ?   40

vi.

Christ still was wandering o'er the earth
  Without a place to lay his head ;
He found free welcome at my hearth,
  He shared my cup and broke my bread:
Now, when I hear those steps sublime,
  That bring the other world to this,
My snake-turned nature, sunk in slime,
  Starts sideway with defiant hiss.

vii.

Upon the hour when I was born,
  God said, " Another man shall be,"   50
And the great Maker did not scorn
  Out of himself to fashion me ;

He sunned me with his ripening looks.
    And Heaven's rich instincts in me grew,
As effortless as woodland nooks
    Send violets up and paint them blue.

VIII.

Yes, I who now, with angry tears,
    Am exiled back to brutish clod,
Have borne unquenched for fourscore years
    A spark of the eternal God ;   60
And to what end ?   How yield I back
    The trust for such high uses given ?
Heaven's light hath but revealed a track
    Whereby to crawl away from heaven.

IX. ·

Men think it is an awful sight
    To see a soul just set adrift
On that drear voyage from whose night
    The ominous shadows never lift;
But 'tis more awful to behold
    A helpless infant newly born,   70
Whose little hands unconscious hold
    The keys of darkness and of morn.

X.

Mine held them once ; I flung away
    Those keys that might have open set
The golden sluices of the day.
    But clutch the keys of darkness yet;

I hear the reapers singing go
 Into God's harvest; I, that might
With them have chosen, here below
 Grope shuddering at the gates of night.

XI.

O glorious Youth, that once wast mine!
 O high Ideal! all in vain
Ye enter at this ruined shrine
 Whence worship ne'er shall rise again;
The bat and owl inhabit here,
 The snake nests in the altar-stone,
The sacred vessels moulder near,
 The image of the God is gone.

A PARABLE.

I.

SAID Christ our Lord, " I will go and see
How the men, my brethren, believe in me."
He passed not again through the gate of birth,
But made himself known to the children of earth.

II.

Then said the chief priests, and rulers, and kings,
" Behold, now, the Giver of all good things;
Go to, let us welcome with pomp and state
Him who alone is mighty and great."

III.

With carpets of gold the ground they spread
Wherever the Son of Man should tread,   10
And in palace-chambers lofty and rare
They lodged him, and served him with kingly fare.

IV.

Great organs surged through arches dim
Their jubilant floods in praise of him;
And in church, and palace, and judgment-hall,
He saw his own image high over all.

V.

But still, wherever his steps they led,
The Lord in sorrow bent down his head,
And from under the heavy foundation-stones,
The son of Mary heard bitter groans.   20

VI.

And in church, and palace, and judgment-hall,
He marked great fissures that rent the wall,
And opened wider and yet more wide
As the living foundation heaved and sighed.

VII.

" Have ye founded your thrones and altars, then,
On the bodies and souls of living men?
And think ye that building shall endure,
Which shelters the noble and crushes the poor?

VIII.

" With gates of silver and bars of gold
Ye have fenced my sheep from their Father's fold ;   30
I have heard the dropping of their tears
In heaven these eighteen hundred years."

IX.

" O Lord and Master, not ours the guilt,
We build but as our fathers built ;
Behold thine images, how they stand,
Sovereign and sole, through all our land.

X.

" Our task is hard, — with sword and flame
To hold thine earth forever the same,
And with sharp crooks of steel to keep
Still, as thou leftest them, thy sheep."   40

XI.

Then Christ sought out an artisan,
A low-browed, stunted, haggard man,
And a motherless girl, whose fingers thin
Pushed from her faintly want and sin.

XII.

These set he in the midst of them,
And as they drew back their garment-hem,
For fear of defilement, " Lo, here," said he,
" The images ye have made of me ! "

SONNETS.

I.

TO A. C. L.

THROUGH suffering and sorrow thou hast passed
To show us what a woman true may be :
They have not taken sympathy from thee,
Nor made thee any other than thou wast,
Save as some tree, which, in a sudden blast,
Sheddeth those blossoms, that are weakly grown,
Upon the air, but keepeth every one
Whose strength gives warrant of good fruit at last :
So thou hast shed some blooms of gayety,
But never one of steadfast cheerfulness;   10
Nor hath thy knowledge of adversity
Robbed thee of any faith in happiness,
But rather cleared thine inner eyes to see
How many simple ways there are to bless.

1840.

II.

WHAT were I, Love, if I were stripped of thee,
If thine eyes shut me out whereby I live,
Thou, who unto my calmer soul dost give
Knowledge, and Truth, and holy Mystery,
Wherein Truth mainly lies for those who see
Beyond the earthly and the fugitive,   20
Who in the grandeur of the soul believe,

And only in the Infinite are free ?
Without thee I were naked, bleak, and bare
As yon dead cedar on the sea-cliff's brow ;
And Nature's teachings, which come to me now,
Common and beautiful as light and air,
Would be as fruitless as a stream which still
Slips through the wheel of some old ruined mill.
1841.

III.

I would not have this perfect love of ours
Grow from a single root, a single stem,
Bearing no goodly fruit, but only flowers
That idly hide life's iron diadem :
It should grow alway like that Eastern tree
Whose limbs take root and spread forth constantly ;
That love for one, from which there doth not spring
Wide love for all, is but a worthless thing.
Not in another world, as poets prate,
Dwell we apart above the tide of things,
High floating o'er earth's clouds on faery wings ;
But our pure love doth ever elevate
Into a holy bond of brotherhood
All earthly things, making them pure and good.
1840.

IV.

" For this true nobleness I seek in vain,
In woman and in man I find it not ;
I almost weary of my earthly lot,

My life-springs are dried up with burning pain."
Thou find'st it not ?   I pray thee look again,
Look *inward* through the depths of thine own soul.
How is it with thee ?   Art thou sound and whole ?
Doth narrow search show thee no earthly stain ?   50
BE NOBLE ! and the nobleness that lies
In other men, sleeping, but never dead,
Will rise in majesty to meet thine own;
Then wilt thou see it gleam in many eyes,
Then will pure light around thy path be shed,
And thou wilt nevermore be sad and lone.
  1840.

V.

TO THE SPIRIT OF KEATS.

GREAT soul, thou sittest with me in my room,
Uplifting me with thy vast, quiet eyes,
On whose full orbs, with kindly lustre, lies
The twilight warmth of ruddy ember-gloom :   60
Thy clear, strong tones will oft bring sudden bloom
Of hope secure, to him who lonely cries,
Wrestling with the young poet's agonies,
Neglect and scorn, which seem a certain doom :
Yes ! the few words which, like great thunder-drops,
Thy large heart down to earth shook doubtfully,
Thrilled by the inward lightning of its might,
Serene and pure, like gushing joy of light,
Shall track the eternal chords of Destiny,
After the moon-led pulse of ocean stops.   70
  1841.

VI.

GREAT Truths are portions of the soul of man;
Great souls are portions of Eternity;
Each drop of blood that e'er through true heart ran
With lofty message, ran for thee and me;
For God's law, since the starry song began,
Hath been, and still forevermore must be,
That every deed which shall outlast Time's span
Must spur the soul to be erect and free;
Slave is no word of deathless lineage sprung;
Too many noble souls have thought and died,   80
Too many mighty poets lived and sung,
And our good Saxon, from lips purified
With martyr-fire, throughout the world hath run
Too long to have God's holy cause denied.

1841.

VII.

I ASK not for those thoughts, that sudden leap
From being's sea, like the isle-seeming Kraken,
With whose great rise the ocean all is shaken
And a heart-tremble quivers through the deep;
Give me that growth which some perchance deem sleep,
Wherewith the steadfast coral-stems uprise,   90
Which, by the toil of gathering energies,
Their upward way into clear sunshine keep,
Until, by Heaven's sweetest influences,
Slowly and slowly spreads a speck of green
Into a pleasant island in the seas,

Where, mid tall palms, the cane-roofed home is seen,
And wearied men shall sit at sunset's hour,
Hearing the leaves and loving God's dear power.
1841.

VIII.

TO M. W. ON HER BIRTHDAY.

MAIDEN, when such a soul as thine is born,
The morning-stars their ancient music make　　　100
And, joyful, once again their song awake,
Long silent now with melancholy scorn;
And thou, not mindless of so blest a morn,
By no least deed its harmony shalt break,
But shalt to that high chime thy footsteps take,
Through life's most darksome passes unforlorn;
Therefore from thy pure faith thou shalt not fall,
Therefore shalt thou be ever fair and free,
And in thine every motion musical
As summer air, majestic as the sea,　　　110
A mystery to those who creep and crawl
Through Time, and part it from Eternity.
1841.

IX.

My Love, I have no fear that thou shouldst die;
Albeit I ask no fairer life than this
Whose numbering-clock is still thy gentle kiss,
While Time and Peace with hands enlockèd fly, —
Yet care I not where in Eternity
We live and love, well knowing that there is　　.

No backward step for those who feel the bliss
Of Faith as their most lofty yearnings high : 120
Love hath so purified my being's core,
Meseems I scarcely should be startled, even.
To find, some morn. that thou hadst gone before ;
Since, with thy love, this knowledge too was given,
Which each calm day doth strengthen more and more,
That they who love are but one step from Heaven.

1841.

X.

I CANNOT think that thou shouldst pass away,
Whose life to mine is an eternal law,
A piece of nature that can have no flaw,
A new and certain sunrise every day ; 130
But, if thou art to be another ray
About the Sun of Life, and art to live
Free from what part of thee was fugitive,
The debt of Love I will more fully pay,
Not downcast with the thought of thee so high,
But rather raised to be a nobler man,
And more divine in my humanity,
As knowing that the waiting eyes which scan
My life are lighted by a purer being,
And ask high, calm-browed deeds, with it agreeing. 140

1841.

XI.

THERE never yet was flower fair in vain,
Let classic poets rhyme it as they will ;
The seasons toil that it may blow again,

And summer's heart doth feel its every ill;
Nor is a true soul ever born for naught;
Wherever any such hath lived and died,
There hath been something for true freedom wrought,
Some bulwark levelled on the evil side:
Toil on, then, Greatness! thou art in the right,
However narrow souls may call thee wrong;　　　150
Be as thou wouldst be in thine own clear sight,
And so thou shalt be in the world's erelong;
For worldlings cannot, struggle as they may,
From man's great soul one great thought hide away.
1841.

XII.

SUB PONDERE CRESCIT.

The hope of Truth grows stronger, day by day;
I hear the soul of Man around me waking,
Like a great sea, its frozen fetters breaking,
And flinging up to heaven its sunlit spray,
Tossing huge continents in scornful play,
And crushing them, with din of grinding thunder,　　160
That makes old emptinesses stare in wonder;
The memory of a glory passed away
Lingers in every heart, as, in the shell,
Resounds the bygone freedom of the sea,
And every hour new signs of promise tell,
That the great soul shall once again be free,
For high, and yet more high, the murmurs swell
Of inward strife for truth and liberty.
1841.

XIII.

Beloved, in the noisy city here,
The thought of thee can make all turmoil cease ;⁣   170
Around my spirit, folds thy spirit clear
Its still, soft arms, and circles it with peace ;
There is no room for any doubt or fear
In souls so overfilled with love's increase,
There is no memory of the bygone year
But growth in heart's and spirit's perfect ease :
How hath our love, half nebulous at first,
Rounded itself into a full-orbed sun !
How have our lives and wills (as haply erst
They were, ere this forgetfulness begun)   180
Through all their earthly distances outburst,
And melted, like two rays of light, in one !
  1842.

XIV.

ON READING WORDSWORTH'S SONNETS IN DEFENCE OF CAPITAL PUNISHMENT.

As the broad ocean endlessly upheaveth,
With the majestic beating of his heart,
The mighty tides, whereof its rightful part
Each sea-wide bay and little weed receiveth,
So, through his soul who earnestly believeth,
Life from the universal Heart doth flow,
Whereby some conquest of the eternal Woe,
By instinct of God's nature, he achieveth :   190
A fuller pulse of this all-powerful beauty

Into the poet's gulf-like heart doth tide,
And he more keenly feels the glorious duty
Of serving Truth, despised and crucified, —
Happy, unknowing sect or creed, to rest
And feel God flow forever through his breast.

1842.

XV.

THE SAME CONTINUED.

Once hardly in a cycle blossometh
A flower-like soul ripe with the seeds of song,
A spirit foreordained to cope with wrong,
Whose divine thoughts are natural as breath,   200
Who the old Darkness thickly scattereth
With starry words, that shoot prevailing light
Into the deeps, and wither. with the blight
Of serene Truth, the coward heart of Death:
Woe, if such spirit thwart its errand high,
And mock with lies the longing soul of man!
Yet one age longer must true Culture lie,
Soothing her bitter fetters as she can,
Until new messages of love outstart
At the next beating of the infinite Heart.   210

XVI.

THE SAME CONTINUED.

The love of all things springs from love of one;
Wider the soul's horizon hourly grows,
And over it with fuller glory flows

The sky-like spirit of God ; a hope begun
In doubt and darkness 'neath a fairer sun
Cometh to fruitage, if it be of Truth ;
And to the law of meekness, faith, and ruth,
By inward sympathy, shall all be won :
This thou shouldst know, who, from the painted feature
Of shifting Fashion, couldst thy brethren turn　　　220
Unto the love of ever-youthful Nature,
And of a beauty fadeless and eterne ;
And always 'tis the saddest sight to see
An old man faithless in Humanity.

XVII.

THE SAME CONTINUED.

A POET cannot strive for despotism ;
His harp falls shattered ; for it still must be
The instinct of great spirits to be free,
And the sworn foes of cunning barbarism :
He who has deepest searched the wide abysm
Of that life-giving Soul which men call fate,　　　230
Knows that to put more faith in lies and hate
Than truth and love is the true atheism :
Upward the soul forever turns her eyes :
The next hour always shames the hour before ·
One beauty, at its highest, prophesies
That by whose side it shall seem mean and poor
No Godlike thing knows aught of less and less,
But widens to the boundless Perfectness.

XVIII.

THE SAME CONTINUED.

THEREFORE think not the Past is wise alone,
For Yesterday knows nothing of the Best,　　　　240
And thou shalt love it only as the nest
Whence glory-wingèd things to Heaven have flown:
To the great Soul only are all things known;
Present and future are to her as past,
While she in glorious madness doth forecast
That perfect bud, which seems a flower full-blown
To each new Prophet, and yet always opes
Fuller and fuller with each day and hour,
Heartening the soul with odor of fresh hopes,
And longings high, and gushings of wide power,　　　250
Yet never is or shall be fully blown
Save in the forethought of the Eternal One.

XIX.

THE SAME CONCLUDED.

FAR 'yond this narrow parapet of Time,
With eyes uplift, the poet's soul should look
Into the Endless Promise, nor should brook
One prying doubt to shake his faith sublime;
To him the earth is ever in her prime
And dewiness of morning; he can see
Good lying hid, from all eternity,
Within the teeming womb of sin and crime;　　　260
His soul should not be cramped by any bar,

His nobleness should be so Godlike high,
That his least deed is perfect as a star,
His common look majestic as the sky,
And all o'erflooded with a light from far,
Undimmed by clouds of weak mortality.

XX.

TO M. O. S.

Mary, since first I knew thee, to this hour,
My love hath deepened, with my wiser sense
Of what in Woman is to reverence;
Thy clear heart, fresh as e'er was forest-flower,   270
Still opens more to me its beauteous dower; —
But let praise hush, — Love asks no evidence
To prove itself well-placed; we know not whence
It gleans the straws that thatch its humble bower:
We can but say we found it in the heart,
Spring of all sweetest thoughts, arch foe of blame,
Sower of flowers in the dusty mart,
Pure vestal of the poet's holy flame, —
This is enough, and we have done our part
If we but keep it spotless as it came.   280

1842.

XXI.

Our love is not a fading, earthly flower:
Its wingèd seed dropped down from Paradise,
And, nursed by day and night, by sun and shower,
Doth momently to fresher beauty rise:

To us the leafless autumn is not bare,
Nor winter's rattling boughs lack lusty green.
Our summer hearts make summer's fulness, where
No leaf, or bud, or blossom may be seen :
For nature's life in love's deep life doth lie,
Love, — whose forgetfulness is beauty's death,   250
Whose mystic key these cells of Thou and I
Into the infinite freedom openeth,
And makes the body's dark and narrow grate
The wide-flung leaves of Heaven's own palace-gate.
    1842.

XXII.

IN ABSENCE.

THESE rugged, wintry days I scarce could bear,
Did I not know, that, in the early spring,
When wild March winds upon their errands sing,
Thou wouldst return, bursting on this still air,
Like those same winds, when, startled from their lair,
They hunt up violets, and free swift brooks   300
From icy cares, even as thy clear looks
Bid my heart bloom, and sing, and break all care :
When drops with welcome rain the April day,
My flowers shall find their April in thine eyes,
Save there the rain in dreamy clouds doth stay,
As loath to fall out of those happy skies ;
Yet sure, my love, thou art most like to May,
That comes with steady sun when April dies.
    1843.

XXIII.

WENDELL PHILLIPS.

HE stood upon the world's broad threshold ; wide
The din of battle and of slaughter rose ;   310
He saw God stand upon the weaker side,
That sank in seeming loss before its foes :
Many there were who made great haste and sold
Unto the cunning enemy their swords,
He scorned their gifts of fame, and power, and gold,
And, underneath their soft and flowery words,
Heard the cold serpent hiss ; therefore he went
And humbly joined him to the weaker part,
Fanatic named, and fool, yet well content
So he could be the nearer to God's heart,   320
And feel its solemn pulses sending blood
Through all the wide-spread veins of endless good.

XXIV.

THE STREET.

THEY pass me by like shadows, crowds on crowds,
Dim ghosts of men, that hover to and fro,
Hugging their bodies round them like thin shrouds
Wherein their souls were buried long ago :
They trampled on their youth, and faith, and love,
They cast their hope of human-kind away,
With Heaven's clear messages they madly strove,
And conquered, — and their spirits turned to clay :   330
Lo ! how they wander round the world, their grave,

Whose ever-gaping maw by such is fed,
Gibbering at living men, and idly rave,
" We, only, truly live, but ye are dead."
Alas ! poor fools, the anointed eye may trace
A dead soul's epitaph in every face !

XXV.

I GRIEVE not that ripe Knowledge takes away
The charm that Nature to my childhood wore,
For, with that insight, cometh, day by day,
A greater bliss than wonder was before ;   340
The real doth not clip the poet's wings, —
To win the secret of a weed's plain heart
Reveals some clew to spiritual things,
And stumbling guess becomes firm-footed art :
Flowers are not flowers unto the poet's eyes,
Their beauty thrills him by an inward sense ;
He knows that outward seemings are but lies,
Or, at the most, but earthly shadows. whence
The soul that looks within for truth may guess
The presence of some wondrous heavenliness.   350

XXVI.

TO J. R. GIDDINGS.

GIDDINGS, far rougher names than thine have grown
Smoother than honey on the lips of men ;
And thou shalt aye be honorably known,
As one who bravely used his tongue and pen,
As best befits a freeman, — even for those

To whom our Law's unblushing front denies
A right to plead against the lifelong woes
Which are the Negro's glimpse of Freedom's skies:
Fear nothing, and hope all things, as the Right
Alone may do securely; every hour   360
The thrones of Ignorance and ancient Night
Lose somewhat of their long usurpèd power,
And Freedom's lightest word can make them shiver
With a base dread that clings to them forever.

XXVII.

I THOUGHT our love at full, but I did err;
Joy's wreath drooped o'er mine eyes; I could not see
That sorrow in our happy world must be
Love's deepest spokesman and interpreter:
But, as a mother feels her child first stir
Under her heart, so felt I instantly   370
Deep in my soul another bond to thee
Thrill with that life we saw depart from her;
O mother of our angel child! twice dear!
Death knits as well as parts, and still, I wis,
Her tender radiance shall infold us here,
Even as the light, borne up by inward bliss,
Threads the void glooms of space without a fear,
To print on farthest stars her pitying kiss.

L'ENVOI.

WHETHER my heart hath wiser grown or not,
In these three years, since I to thee inscribed,   380

Mine own betrothed, the firstlings of my muse, —
Poor windfalls of unripe experience,
Young buds plucked hastily by childish hands
Not patient to await more full-blown flowers, —
At least it hath seen more of life and men,
And pondered more, and grown a shade more sad ;
Yet with no loss of hope or settled trust
In the benignness of that Providence
Which shapes from out our elements awry
The grace and order that we wonder at,   390
The mystic harmony of right and wrong,
Both working out His wisdom and our good :
A trust, Beloved, chiefly learned of thee,
Who hast that gift of patient tenderness,
The instinctive wisdom of a woman's heart.
They tell us that our land was made for song,
With its huge rivers and sky-piercing peaks,
Its sealike lakes and mighty cataracts,
Its forests vast and hoar, and prairies wide,
And mounds that tell of wondrous tribes extinct.   400
But Poesy springs not from rocks and woods ;
Her womb and cradle are the human heart,
And she can find a nobler theme for song
In the most loathsome man that blasts the sight
Than in the broad expanse of sea and shore
Between the frozen deserts of the poles.
All nations have their message from on high,
Each the messiah of some central thought,
For the fulfilment and delight of Man :

One has to teach that labor is divine;   410
Another Freedom; and another Mind;
And all, that God is open-eyed and just,
The happy centre and calm heart of all.

Are, then, our woods, our mountains, and our streams,
Needful to teach our poets how to sing?
O maiden rare, far other thoughts were ours,
When we have sat by ocean's foaming marge,
And watched the waves leap roaring on the rocks,
Than young Leander and his Hero had,
Gazing from Sestos to the other shore.   420
The moon looks down and ocean worships her,
Stars rise and set, and seasons come and go
Even as they did in Homer's elder time,
But we behold them not with Grecian eyes:
Then they were types of beauty and of strength,
But now of freedom, unconfined and pure,
Subject alone to Order's higher law.
What cares the Russian serf or Southern slave
Though we should speak as man spake never yet
Of gleaming Hudson's broad magnificence,   430
Or green Niagara's never-ending roar?
Our country hath a gospel of her own
To preach and practise before all the world, —
The freedom·and divinity of man,
The glorious claims of human brotherhood, —
Which to pay nobly, as a freeman should,
Gains the sole wealth that will not fly away, —

And the soul's fealty to none but God.
These are realities, which make the shows
Of outward Nature, be they ne'er so grand,   440
Seem small, and worthless, and contemptible.
These are the mountain-summits for our bards,
Which stretch far upward into heaven itself,
And give such wide-spread and exulting view
Of hope, and faith, and onward destiny,
That shrunk Parnassus to a molehill dwindles.
Our new Atlantis, like a morning-star,
Silvers the mirk face of slow-yielding Night,
The herald of a fuller truth than yet
Hath gleamed upon the upraised face of Man   450
Since the earth glittered in her stainless prime, —
Of a more glorious sunrise than of old
Drew wondrous melodies from Memnon huge,
Yea, draws them still, though now he sit waist-deep
In the ingulfing flood of whirling sand,
And look across the wastes of endless gray,
Sole wreck, where once his hundred-gated Thebes
Pained with her mighty hum the calm, blue heaven ;
Shall the dull stone pay grateful orisons,
And we till noonday bar the splendor out,   460
Lest it reproach and chide our sluggard hearts,
Warm-nestled in the down of Prejudice,
And be content, though clad with angel-wings,
Close-clipped, to hop about from perch to perch,
In paltry cages of dead men's dead thoughts ?
O, rather, like the skylark, soar and sing,

And let our gushing songs befit the dawn
And sunrise, and the yet unshaken dew
Brimming the chalice of each full-blown hope.
Whose blithe front turns to greet the growing day! 470
Never had poets such high call before,
Never can poets hope for higher one,
And, if they be but faithful to their trust,
Earth will remember them with love and joy
And O, far better, God will not forget.
For he who settles Freedom's principles,
Writes the death-warrant of all tyranny;
Who speaks the truth stabs Falsehood to the heart,
And his mere word makes despots tremble more
Than ever Brutus with his dagger could. 480
Wait for no hints from waterfalls or woods,
Nor dream that tales of red men, brute and fierce,
Repay the finding of this Western World,
Or needed half the globe to give them birth:
Spirit supreme of Freedom! not for this
Did great Columbus tame his eagle soul
To jostle with the daws that perch in courts;
Not for this, friendless, on an unknown sea,
Coping with mad waves and more mutinous spirits,
Battled he with the dreadful ache at heart 490
Which tempts, with devilish subtleties of doubt,
The hermit of that loneliest solitude,
The silent desert of a great New Thought;
Though loud Niagara were to-day struck dumb,
Yet would this cataract of boiling life

Rush plunging on and on to endless deeps.
And utter thunder till the world shall cease, —
A thunder worthy of the poet's song,
And which alone can fill it with true life.
The high evangel to our country granted   500
Could make apostles, yea, with tongues of fire,
Of hearts half-darkened back again to clay!
'Tis the soul only that is national,
And he who pays true loyalty to that
Alone can claim the wreath of patriotism.

   Beloved! if I wander far and oft
From that which I believe, and feel, and know,
Thou wilt forgive, not with a sorrowing heart,
But with a strengthened hope of better things;
Knowing that I, though often blind and false   510
To those I love, and O, more false than all
Unto myself, have been most true to thee,
And that whoso in one thing hath been true
Can be as true in all.   Therefore thy hope
May yet not prove unfruitful, and thy love
Meet, day by day, with less unworthy thanks,
Whether, as now, we journey hand in hand,
Or, parted in the body, yet are one
In spirit and the love of holy things.

NOTES AND QUESTIONS.

THE VISION OF SIR LAUNFAL.

PRELUDE TO PART I.

STANZA I. In what frame is the organist's mind as he begins the melody?

Compare the fourth line with the first line of stanza i. of Browning's "Abt Vogler."

What serves to render the musician's theme more distinct and clear?

Explain the metaphor in the seventh and eighth lines.

Questions to be noted after studying the Poem.

What connection has the first stanza with the rest of the poem?

Would the conclusion that Lowell had no conception of his theme and its development when he began to write be necessarily correct? Give reasons.

Might this stanza be termed a metaphor, in which the organist stands for the poet, the instrument for the mechanical part of the poetry, and the theme of the music for the theme of the poem?

Is this revery as an introduction better suited to the subject and its handling than an abrupt one would be? Why?

Why is this " musical " figure particularly apt?

STANZA II. Compare the first two lines with the ninth line of stanza v. of Wordsworth's " Intimations of Immortality ": —

" Heaven lies about us in our infancy."

Could any other word be substituted for " splendors " in the second line and give the thought as well?

Explain the figure in the fourth line: " We Sinais climb."

It was upon Mount Sinai that God talked with Moses and gave the Ten Commandments and the Law. The Israelites were in the third month of their journey out of Egypt. Mount Sinai is in the northwestern part of Arabia. (Exodus xix. and xx.)

What clause in the third line explains why "we know it not"?

Upon what condition does the acquirement of truth by the mind rest? (Cf. St. John vii. 17.)

STANZA III. What figures are to be found in this stanza?

From what have our lives "fallen"? To what are our lives "traitor"?

Druidism was the religion of the ancient Celts. The priests, the Druids, dwelt in the woods, and there offered their sacrifices, interpreted to the people the divine will, and exercised over them the authority of judges, prophets, and teachers.

Compare the second, third, seventh, and eighth lines for similarity of thought with the seventh and eighth lines of stanza iii. of the "Intimations of Immortality": —

> "The cataracts blow their trumpets from the steep,
> No more shall grief of mine the season wrong."

Why does Lowell represent the "druid wood" as uttering the benedicite, rather than the winds, or the sea?

With what are the weakness and selfishness of man contrasted?

STANZA IV. What two thoughts are opposed to each other in this stanza?

What is the nature of the things which earth "sells" us?

In what coin do we pay?

What line suggests the satisfaction we receive from these bargains?

Explain the figures in the seventh and eighth lines.

What is the nature of the things which God gives us?

STANZA V. What makes the beauty of this stanza?

Explain the figure in the third and fourth lines, and point out its significance.

To the poet's mind, what natural relation exists between earth and heaven? What line suggests the answer?

Why is the buttercup, rather than the clover, or violet, spoken of as "catching the sun in its chalice"?

What figure, in the description of the bird, adds to the effect of the summer grace and lightsomeness of the picture?

Is the use of the word "deluge," in the twentieth line, a happy one artistically? Give reasons for your answer.

Why have we the expression "*dumb* breast" in the twenty-second line?

What instinct urges her to sing?

In what sense is the word "nice" used in the twenty-fourth line?

STANZA VI. What figure is used in the first four lines? How is the sense of largeness imparted by the source of the figure?

Does the figurative mode of expression used from the thirteenth to the eighteenth lines add to, or detract from, the beauty of the thought? Why?

Where before has the breeze been spoken of as bearing messages?

Explain the figure in the twenty-second line.

Note that in stanzas v. and vi., Lowell, even as Wordsworth, conceives of Nature as having a thoughtful, conscious life: —

> "Every clod feels a stir of might,
>   And, groping blindly above it for light,
>   Climbs to a *soul* in grass and flowers."

> "The little bird sits at his door in the sun,
>   Atilt like a blossom among the leaves,
>   And lets his illumined being o'errun
>   With the deluge of summer it receives;
>   His mate feels the eggs beneath her wings,
>   And the heart in her dumb breast flutters and sings;
>   He sings to the wide world, and she to her nest."

> "The breeze comes whispering in our ear,
>   That the robin is plastering his house hard by."

STANZA VII. In Lowell's mind, what feeling exists between Man and Nature? What influence has the latter upon him? Let the student find instances in the poem thus far, illustrating this thought.

Explain the figure in the eighth line.

Why is the work wrought by sin and sorrow aptly likened to the rifts of the volcanic crater?

What lines express the purpose of the Prelude, and somewhat suggest the story which is to follow?

STANZA I. **The Holy Grail.** The cup of emerald from which Christ drank at the last supper. Joseph of Arimathea caught in it some of the blood of Christ at the crucifixion. According to the earliest legend, "Le Petit Saint-Graal," the cup was taken to the West by the brother-in-law of Joseph of Arimathea; a later one, "Le Grand-Saint-Graal," relates that Joseph himself took it to England. The Celtic stories connected with King Arthur became blended with those of the Grail. A search for the Grail was instituted among the Knights of the Round Table. Only he whose life was pure and stainless might hope to see the blessed cup. To Galahad was the vision granted.

Compare the preparations made for the search by Sir Launfal with those made by Percivale's sister, and Sir Galahad, in Tennyson's "Holy Grail:" stanza viii., lines nine and ten; stanza ix., lines thirteen and fourteen; and stanza xv., line thirteen.

Why is the figure in the twelfth line most fitting?

When before has the divine Voice come to men in cloud and dream? (Judges vii. 13; Daniel ii. and iv.; Joel ii. 28; St. Matthew ii. 12, 13. St. Matthew xvii. 5.)

STANZA II. What line decides one that here is described a midsummer *morning?*

Why does not the castle add to the picture of summer fulness and joy?

What figure is there within the simile of the sixth and seventh lines expressed by the words, "outpost of winter"?

(The castle, symbolic of feudal times, when sharp lines marked the divisions of society, and chilled the feeling of the brotherhood of man, even as in winter Nature is cold and unresponsive, — stands as an outpost of whatever remains that would separate man from his neighbor; observing with jealous glance the enemy which it sees in the tendency to break down caste, figured in the lavish generosity, and blending of the summer life.)

Why has the poet used the ancient mode of spelling in "countree"?

What are the "pavilions" of summer referred to in the fourteenth line?

What common occurrence has the poet noticed in the last line?

STANZA III. By what poetical artifice is the music of the first two lines produced? Notice the frequent use of the same throughout the entire poem.

What figure used in the second stanza is continued in the third?

Why does the use of this figure add to the effectiveness of the description?

What serves to render the tenth and eleventh lines melodious?

In what spirit does Sir Launfal start out in his search for the Holy Grail?

What is his motive in the search? (See the closing lines of the Prelude to Part I.) Do you find any hint so far that there is aught of holy desire and longing to see the Grail?

STANZA IV. What contrast is there in this stanza?

How does the castle " rebuff " the gifts of the sunshine?

Why could it not live its life of isolation without affecting its surroundings either one way or the other?

Explain the figure in the sixth and seventh lines.

STANZA V. What is the meaning and significance of the expression, " made morn through the darksome gate " ?

What effect does the leper produce upon Sir Launfal?

What clause emphasizes the abased attitude of the leper's mind?

What is the force of the simile in its application in the seventh and eighth lines?

What is Sir Launfal's motive in giving the gold to the beggar?

STANZA VI. Why does the leper refuse the gift?

With what does he contrast the gold?

How does he characterize that which is given from a sense of duty?

Meaning of " gives to that which is out of sight " ?

Compare the fifth line with Luke xi. 41 (Revised Version).

What is the source of all beauty?

What is the " thread which runs through all and doth all unite " ?

What is the largeness of such a gift, though it be " but a slender mite " ?

Why does he say that " a god goes with it " ?

PRELUDE TO PART II.

STANZA I.   What change in Nature is now introduced?

wold = an unwooded country (whether a plain or hill).

What is the first touch by which the picture is relieved of its intense coldness and loneliness?

groin = the projecting, solid angle formed by the meeting of two vaults, growing more obtuse as it approaches the summit.

What makes the beauty of the simile in the twefth and thirteenth lines?

Does the introduction of the word " *steel*-stemmed " into this picture of Nature strengthen, or weaken, the desired effect?   Why?

arabesque = a style of ornamentation consisting of a pattern in which plants, fruits, and figures of men and animals are fantastically interlaced.

What attribute of heaven is mentioned?

Note the attractive way in which personification is used; or, rather, the active, joyous life with which the poet invests Nature even in winter.

What would you say of Lowell's attitude toward Nature?   Give instances in the poem to substantiate your answer.

Notice the frequent use of alliteration in this Prelude.

What lines indicate the models from which the brook-builder fashioned his house?

In this use of personification of the frost-builder, is the poet quite consistent?   Note and compare the eighth line with the thirty-seventh?

What is there in the latter half of the stanza to soften the winter severity?

STANZA II.   By what figure is the merriment of Christmas heightened?

corbel = a bracket used in architecture to support the spring of an arch; much used in the Gothic style of architecture.   A common form consists of a series of stones or bricks, each projecting slightly beyond the one below it.

Yule-log = a large log of wood, formerly put on the hearth on Christmas Eve as the foundation of the fire.   It was brought in with much ceremony.

pennon = a flag or streamer.

to belly = to swell out.

Name the different figures used in this stanza.

Note the device by which the musical effect of the last four lines is gained.

What effect upon the outer cold does this glimpse of Christmas warmth and cheer make?

Why does the poet, even in this stanza, but briefly allude to the "song and laughter," and then turn to the pictures and reveries suggested by the Yule-log's tongues of fire and scattering sparks?

STANZA III. What sounds are introduced into this stanza? With what are they contrasted in the preceding stanza?

Notice the metaphor in the second line. What is there in the season of the year to render the wind's Christmas carol especially sad?

seneschal = an officer in the houses of princes and dignitaries, in the Middle Ages, who had the superintendence of feasts and domestic ceremonies.

What effect does the voice of the seneschal have upon Sir Launfal? What figure conveys this idea?

How is his loneliness affected by the nearness of the hall in which are "song and laughter"?

PART II.

STANZA I. Compare the metaphor, "the river's shroud," with the metaphor in the first stanza, lines eight and nine, of the Prelude to this Part. What is the difference in the effect of the two?

What kind of a sky would one imagine for such a morning?

What is the poet's reason for giving us here a morning so different from the one in Part I.?

What is the most forcible impression made by the stanza? What lines convey it?

STANZA II. What figure is there in the first line?

surcoat = a long, flowing garment of knights, worn over the armor, and often emblazoned with the arms of the wearer.

Why was not Sir Launfal disturbed by the loss of his earldom?

Was he not in greater need of home and comfort than when he started out in his search for the Grail?

What lines indicate that there had grown into his heart a genuine sympathy for suffering and sorrow?

STANZA III. What word may be substituted for "idle" in the second line?

Explain the figure in this line.

To what do the words "black and small" refer in the eighth line?

Why does Sir Launfal gain more comfort in the "light and warmth of long ago," than in the sight of the ruddy glow sent out from the "great hall fire"?

What renders the picture of the "little spring" so attractive?

STANZA IV. What interrupts his revery of the past?

What line marks a difference in Sir Launfal's attitude toward the leper as contrasted with that of the first time he saw him in the vision?

What constitutes the peculiar horror of the disease of leprosy?

Explain the significance of the simile in lines five and six.

STANZA V. Whom does Sir Launfal see in the leper?

Had it taken him a long, or a short time, even in the vision, to come to that state where he could behold the Christ in every fellow-being?

Whom is he addressing in the last two lines?

Cf. the last line with St. Matthew xxv. 40.

STANZA VI. Cf. with the first line the first line of stanza vi., Part I. How is the difference in the attitude of the leper to be explained?

"**straightway he.**" To whom does the pronoun refer?

Do you agree with the poet in thinking that the heart of Sir Launfal was "ashes and dust"? In what sense does Lowell mean it?

What was Sir Launfal's gift to the leper when he first met him?

What is it now?

Why does the leper spurn the gold in Part I., but here accept the "mouldy crust" and the icy water as "fine wheaten bread" and "red wine"?

Does Sir Launfal give the whole of his crust to the leper?

Would it have been better had he done so?

Notice later the spiritual lesson Lowell would teach.

What figure is used in the last two lines?

What change do we find in "the soul that was starving in darkness before"? See Part I., stanza vi.

Note the use of alliteration in this stanza.

STANZA VII. Into whom is the leper transformed?

Is this metaphor in which Christ is likened to a gate original with the poet? (St. John x. 7.)

Cf. with the miracle which took place at the Beautiful gate of the Temple, recorded in Acts iii. 1–8.

STANZA VIII. Why are the leaves of the pine used, rather than those of some other tree?

What is the force of the simile in the second and third lines?

What need might there be for the first words of the Voice?

Although in the many years, Sir Launfal had failed to find the Holy Grail, why do you think the search had not been wholly "without avail"?

What significance lies in the fact that it was at his own door, rather than in some distant clime, that he found the Grail at last?

Compare the first use of the Holy Grail with the service rendered by Sir Launfal by which his search is rewarded.

What is the kernel of the thought in the last six lines?

Does modern charity fulfil the requirement of these lines? Give reasons for your answer.

Compare these obligations which are laid by Lowell upon the soul with those which Christ lays upon us. (St. John xv. 12, 13.)

How is it that when the gift is prompted by the true spirit, not only Christ, and the "hungering neighbor," are fed, but the act serves as food to the giver also?

Why is it impossible for the human soul to be satisfied in a selfish life?

STANZA IX. What beside the dream did Sir Launfal feel that the sleep had brought him?

Does Lowell evidently think that God speaks to us through our "higher instincts" and intuitions as well as through the Scriptures?

What is the "stronger mail" referred to in the fifth line?

What idea is expressed by the use of the auxiliary verb in this line?

STANZA X. By what figure is the hospitality with which all are welcomed to the castle emphasized?

What change is introduced in this stanza into the picture of the castle as given us in the second stanza of Part I.?

Is the figure from the fifth to the tenth lines a new one?

Was it necessary that Summer should enter the castle in disguise?

What shows that Sir Launfal had truly learned the lesson of the vision?

How did he show it in his life?

SUMMARY.

Are the words mostly of Latin, or Anglo-Saxon origin?

What is the most common device by which the melodious effect of the poem is produced?

From what source is the majority of the figures drawn?

Is the poet consistent throughout in the structure of the verse?

Is the setting of each Part in harmony with the thought?

Comparing the poem with Tennyson's " Holy Grail," which would you consider the greater? Give reasons.

What is the central thought of each?

From this poem, would one conclude that Lowell agrees with that philosopher who defined love as " unity of life"?

The Students' Series of English Classics.

DURABLY AND HANDSOMELY BOUND IN CLOTH AND CHEAP IN PRICE.

SOME OF THE BOOKS.

Most of them required for Admission to College.

Bates's Ballad Books.	50 cents
Burke's Speech on Conciliation with America	35 "
Carlyle's Essay on Burns	35 "
Carlyle's Diamond Necklace	35 "
Coleridge's Ancient Mariner	25 "
De Quincey's Revolt of the Tartars	35 "
De Quincey's Joan of Arc and other selections	35 "
Dryden's Palamon and Arcite	
George Eliot's Silas Marner	35 "
Goldsmith's Traveler and Deserted Village	25 "
Goldsmith's Vicar of Wakefield	50 "
Johnson's History of Rasselas	35 "
Longfellow's Evangeline	35 "
Lowell's Vision of Sir Launfal	
Matthew Arnold's Sohrab and Rustum	25 "
Macaulay's Essay on Lord Clive	35 "
Macaulay's Second Essay on the Earl of Chatham . . .	35 "
Macaulay's Essays on Milton and Addison	35 "
Macaulay's Life of Samuel Johnson	25 "
Macaulay's Lays of Ancient Rome	
Milton's Paradise Lost, Books I and II	35 "
Milton's L'Allegro, Il Penseroso, Comus, and Lycidas . . .	25 "
Pope's Iliad, Books I, VI, XXII, and XXIV	35 "
Scott's Marmion	35 "
Scott's Lady of the Lake	35 "
Scudder's Introduction to Writings of John Ruskin	50 "
Shakespeare's A Midsummer Night's Dream	35 "
Shakespeare's As You Like It	35 "
Shakespeare's Macbeth	35 "
Shakespeare's Merchant of Venice	35 "
Sir Roger de Coverley Papers from the *Spectator*	35 "
Thomas's Selections from Washington Irving	50 "
Tennyson's Elaine	25 "
Tennyson's Princess	35 "
Webster's First Bunker Hill Oration	25 "

Any of the above books sent postpaid on receipt of price. Usual discount on quantities. Correspondence Solicited.

LEACH, SHEWELL & SANBORN, Publishers,

BOSTON.   NEW YORK.   CHICAGO.

The Students' Series of English Classics.

EMINENT SCHOLARSHIP
COMBINED WITH LARGE BUSINESS EXPERIENCE.

SOME OF THE EDITORS.

Frank T. Baker, Teachers' College, New York City.
Katharine Lee Bates, Wellesley College.
Henry H. Belfield, Chicago Manual Training School.
Henry W. Boynton, Phillips Andover Academy.
Gamaliel Bradford, Jr., Instructor in Literature.
James Chalmers, Wisconsin Normal School.
Albert S. Cook, Yale University.
W. W. Curtis, Principal of High School, Pawtucket, R. I.
Warren F. Gregory, High School, Hartford, Conn.
Louise M. Hodgkins, late of Wellesley College.
Fannie M. McCauley, Winchester School, Baltimore.
W. A. Mozier, High School, Ottawa, Ill.
Mary Harriott Norris, Instructor in Literature.
F. V. N. Painter, Roanoke College.
D. D. Pratt, High School, Portsmouth, Ohio.
Warwick J. Price, St. Paul's School.
J. G. Riggs, School Superintendent, Plattsburg, N.Y.
A. S. Roe, late Principal of High School, Worcester, Mass.
Fred N. Scott, University of Michigan.
Vida D. Scudder, Wellesley College.
L. Dupont Syle, University of California.
Isaac Thomas, Principal of High School, New Haven, Conn.
James Arthur Tufts, Phillips Exeter Academy.
William K. Wickes, Principal of High School, Syracuse, N.Y.
Mabel C. Willard, Instructor, New Haven, Conn.

LEACH, SHEWELL & SANBORN, Publishers,

BOSTON.   NEW YORK.   CHICAGO.